SHEYANNE WARREN

Spied

A Deceptive High Novel

F7P
FOREVER SEVEN PRESS
READ, REVIEW, REPEAT

Contents

Acknowledgments	v
We have no choice	1
Welcome to Deceptive High	5
Speeches	12
Maybe this won't be so bad	17
1st day of class	21
This might actually be fun	28
Ready, set, go	30
Done	34
Hmm?	38
Conflicted and confused	45
Pool Days	48
Pieces of the puzzle	53
Wash Day	57
They're watching you	64
Can you believe this?	69
The Adventure, Adventure	72
They will not beat me	78
You all started here	83
You burned her?!	88
Long overdue	93
Anticipate my next move	98
Next week then?	103
Steroids, really?	106

Blush 109

Minding our business 113

Buzz, stop flirting 115

Drug test 121

Practice what I preach 124

It all makes sense 132

Surprise 137

Halloween 141

The party goes on 146

Behave 150

Here we go 154

I'm late 158

Sibling fighting x10 164

Learned your lessons the hard way 169

Damn 174

Lecture 177

Monica Michelson 179

Fair Trade 181

Back in the day 184

About the Author 189

Acknowledgments

I have been more excited for this novel as I ever been. I loved writing and developing the characters. My mission as an author, a self published author is to write content I care about. My main characters will always be women of color. My characters will always be diverse. I will do my best to write in representation and reality. I truly understand the importance of representation of both people of color and realistic representation of women and I take pride in bringing this form of entertainment to all of you.

I want to first start off by thanking my team; Dream Manson and Shelly Lopez. My book would not be at the point it is without my editor and cover designer. Shelley has been with me since the beginning of my journey and has helped get out the content that my fans have come to love. Dream did an excellent job with my cover. She really captures the essence of my characters and brought them to life.

Secondly, I want to show love to the supporters who's been with my throughout my journey. I truly appreciate all the love and support and am excited to continue my journey with you!

Lastly, thanks to my beta-readers and my launch team. My process would now be complete without you.

We have no choice

J anelle looked at her husband, her brown eyes filling with tears. "What are we going to do? The twins go into high school in two months."

The hard lines on Duante's face hardened. His brown eyes nearly looked black in the light. He looked over at his wife. Her eyes were filled with so much emotion.

"We have no choice Nel. We signed the papers saying our twins would join the Agency's Academy. We can't back out now, they will kill us.. The only reason we decided to live in Charlotte is because Douglas is in Mountain Island."

"I do not want my children living our life. The danger, the lying, the looking over our shoulders. It was hard enough without having to hide my abilities." Fat tears rolled from Janelle's eyes, soaking her chest.

Duante turned his head away from her. Janelle rolled her eyes and wiped her face. Heading over to her vanity, she poured hair cream into her hands and ran it though her natural curls. In a few practiced minutes, her hair was plaited into two French braids.

"We need to enroll them in the boarding school. When they graduate, let's hope they decide to go to college and not follow our lifestyle." Duante whispered tiredly.

Janelle wiped at her face furiously. Picking up a tissue and wiping she walked to the bedroom door. Pausing with her hand on the doorknob she muttered "fine" and then walked out of the room.

* * *

Downstairs, the twins were sitting at the kitchen island.

"Hey Ma," Dion said stuffing his mouth with pizza rolls. He shook his head, moving his shoulder length locs out of his eyes.

"Hi Mother," Lanelle said. "You remember we have that pool party at the Jones' down the street tomorrow. We are spending the night tonight. We can still go right?"

Janelle made herself busy looking in the refrigerator so the kids wouldn't see her tear-filled eyes.

"The Jones who? You mean Tom and Jamie?"

"Yes, Mother," Lanelle whined. "You can't say no. You already said we could go."

"Ma, we asked you weeks ago!" Dion added.

Duante walked into the room, and the kids turned their attention towards their father.

"Yo Dad, I don't know what's wrong with Ma, but she told us we could go to the pool party weeks ago!"

"You better watch who you're talking to, Boy." Duante growled. Janelle got herself together, grabbed the juice, and closed the refrigerator.

Dion lowered his head. "Sorry Sir," he mumbled.

"I remember, you can go. Calm down, you two." She huffed.

"Alright cool" Dion got up and put his dish in the sink. The twins raced for the front door. They skidded to a hault when they heard their father bellow, "Come sit."

The twins groaned and went back to the table.

"We need to talk about high school."

Lanelle's face lit up "Oh, we want to go to Berkeley, please don't send us to Lakeview with all the white people. Berkeley is a good school Mother, and it's more mixed," she rambled on quickly.

Duante looked at Janelle, who was already staring at him. He took a deep breath and turned towards his twins. "We are sending you two to a boarding school."

"Boarding school," they said together in disbelief. "Dad please," Lanelle whined.

"Pops, we want to stay with our friends," Dion joined in.

Duante put up a hand, stopping them. "You two go to the party. When you come back, there is a lot that your mother and I have to tell you."

* * *

When the twins were walking back from the party Lanelle put her wet and kinky shoulder length hair, into a ponytail puff. She sucked her teeth when the hair wouldn't cooperate.

Dion rolled his eyes. "Well, why don't you go oh-natural," he mocked.

Lanelle elbowed him, in the ribs. "Stop mocking me. I want it straight for a few weeks. Then I'm going to get braids put in."

Dion was on his phone, ignoring his sister as she talked about her hair.

"Dion," she said, her voice breaking. "They're going to send us to boarding school."

Dion put his arm around his sister's neck. "Don't go to the worst-case scenario yet. They said they have to talk to us. We still have time to convince them. I don't want to leave our friends, but boarding school could be fun," he said with a shrug.

Lanelle nodded, taking a deep breath. "I don't know how much fun I will have without my friends," she mumbled.

The twins walked in the house, and their parents were in the living room watching TV. Lanelle collapsed in the chair. Dion sat on the arm of the chair, with his hand resting on his sister's back.

Duante turned the TV off and turned towards his kids. He placed his hands over his wife's; he saw she was trembling. "Your mother and I are spies."

Welcome to Deceptive High

L anelle and Dion Sparks stood in front of the Howard building at Douglas High School. It was a large brick building with big white columns in the entry ways.

Boarding school, they were at boarding school. Their parents, Duante and Janelle Sparks, were sending them away.

Lanelle looked up at the building and sighed. She would have to spend the next four years here. It was so unfair. Her parents had signed their life away without giving them any say.

Lanelle had her natural curls straightened. Half of it was pulled back into a ponytail. She wore a gray tank top and simple blue jeans with her favorite pair of wedges. She didn't put on a ton of makeup. Well, her mother didn't let her wear a ton of makeup, but today she only had on mascara and lip gloss.

"Are you going to stare all day or are you going to help?" Dion asked her.

Lanelle sucked her teeth and squinted her eyes. "Shut up," she said. Sighing, she made her way to the car and helped her family gather her and Dion's belongings. As they walked up to the door of Howard Hall, a man and woman stood in the entranceway.

The tall woman with long black hair pulled into a high bun greeted them cheerfully. "Hello Agents Sparks." Her smiling disposition was the opposite of the sour look her mother was wearing.

"Monica, Jason," her mother said, nodding towards both people.

Her father pulled a card out of his pocket. Jason took out a chunky phone and scanned the card. He looked down at the screen and then back up at her parents.

"All set. Welcome to Douglas High," Jason said. The two of them moved to the side to let her family through.

Everyone began to move into the building but Lanelle couldn't believe how rude they were.

"So y'all are going to act like we are not standing here?"

Janelle spun around and glared at her daughter. "Lanelle, you better watch your tone," she said sharply.

"I'm sorry Mother," she muttered. "But that was completely rude of them not to acknowledge us at all." Lanelle turned her attention to Monica and Jason. She extended her hand towards Monica first. "Hello, I'm Lanelle Sparks and I go here now."

Monica shook her hand and grinned. "Hello Lanelle, my name is Monica Michaelson. I am one of the instructors here."

Lanelle turned her attention towards Jason and looked at him expectantly.

Jason grunted and extended his hand to Lanelle. "I'm Jason," he said gruffly.

Lanelle scrunched her face up. *Rude*, she thought. Then she fixed her face into a smile before her mother gave her the 'I'm going to embarrass you if you don't stop' look.

Monica smiled back, and Lanelle squeezed past her to follow her family. Walking through the halls, Dion was making himself at home already. Saying 'what's up' to people and smiling at the girls. That's one thing she loved about her brother. He was so charming and people loved him.

She just wished they'd loved her too.

Once they got to the end of an extremely long hall, Dion and her parents stopped in front of a door.

"This is it," her father enthused.

"You know what Pops? I'm kinda' feeling this whole spy school thing."

Lanelle sucked her teeth. "Well, that makes one of us then," she mumbled.

Dion put his arm around her. "Come on sis. Let's make the best out of this situation. What's the worst that can happen, instead of us becoming bad ass super spies?"

The family entered the room and Duante looked back at his son with his eyebrow raised. "I hear you curse again, I'm going to embarrass you."

Dion lowered his head. "Yes Sir."

Once his father turned his head, he smirked at Lanelle.

Dion's room was big. He had a roommate who was already there and settled in. The boy looked up from the folder he was looking at when they entered.

"What's up, I'm Dion. This is my sister Lanelle and my parents."

"I'm Booker." Booker got up and shook Duante's hand and then bowed his head at Janelle saying "ma'am."

"Nice manners," Janelle commented. "Is your family still here?"

Booker sat back on the bed, averting eye contact. "No, ma'am" he said simply.

Lanelle couldn't believe her eyes. She was looking at her future husband. Not only was he fine, he was extra fine. He was in this hellhole with her, and her brother's roommate. Lanelle couldn't believe her luck.

Booker had caramel skin with hazel eyes. His short and curly hair was shaved around the sides. He was the same height at Dion, around five foot six and Lanelle knew she was in love.

She was so entranced with her future husband she didn't realize everyone was looking at her. Dion picked up a pillow and threw it at her. The pillow knocked her in her face.

"Dang Dion," she squealed.

"Don't be rude," her mother interjected. "Booker asked you a question."

Lanelle turned her attention towards Booker. "I'm sorry, what?" she asked. In her head she was screaming, *Be cool, be cool, don't say anything stupid!*

"Do you like being a twin?" he repeated.

"Oh, I like having a brother. I don't know whether I like that particular brother though."

Booker chuckled, and Dion shot her a dirty look. Lanelle stuck her tongue out at her brother.

"Enough" her mother said.

Duante picked up a folder that was on the side table and handed it to Dion.

"This is your entrance packet, Son. Read it. It has the rules and your schedule in it. We are going up to get Lanelle settled. We will be back to say goodbye."

Dion grabbed the folder and tossed it on the bed. "Yeah, no problem Pops," he said as he turned back towards his bags.

* * *

Lanelle and her parents walked back towards the front doors to head upstairs to the girls' unit. Lanelle starts to walk down a hall, and her mother puts her hand on her shoulder. "This way Lanelle."

Lanelle followed her mother through another hall. There weren't as many doors on this part of the hallway.

"Why do I go down here?" Lanelle asked.

"You get a single room." Janelle replied.

"Why?"

"Any student whose parents graduated in the top five of their class gets a single room," Her mother explained.

"So why does Dion have a roommate?"

"Because your mother made Top five, and I didn't," Duante explained. "So, since we have twins and only one of us was Top five, we had to choose. We decided you would benefit more from privacy than Dion."

"Something else you made a decision about without asking me," Lanelle mumbled.

Janelle turned around. "What?"

Lanelle suppressed a groan. "Nothing mother." *How does she always hear me?* Lanelle thought,

They approached Lanelle's door and stopped in front of it.

"Do you want to do the honors?" Her father asked.

"Sure," she sighed.

She walked past her parents and opened the door. The room was plain just like Dion's, she just had all the space to herself. She walked in slow, inspecting everything.

"Here" Janelle said, handing her the duffle bag. Lanelle put the bags down she was holding and took the one from her mother. When she unzipped it, it contained posters and other knick knacks for decorating. The corners of her mouth began to turn up.

"I thought you'd want some things to make it look better," Janelle said.

Lanelle deflated. She was still irritated with her parents, but she loved them and her mother always knew how to make things better, kinda.

"Thanks Mother," she surprised them both by hugging her. Lanelle leaned into her mother, not wanting to let go.

"I'm not sure if I can do this," she whispered into her mother's chest.

Janelle pulled her daughter back by her shoulders so she could look at her. "It won't be easy, but you can do it."

Lanelle looked into her mother's eyes, willing the confidence she saw to sweep into her and fill her body.

"If you feel weird or things start to happen that you don't understand, call me. You hear?" Janelle asked.

Lanelle nodded silently.

"Okay, give me a hug Lanelle," Duante said. "I need you to read your folder, it's over on the bed."

"Okay Father," she said, while hugging him back.

Duante and Janelle left the room. As soon as the door was shut, Duante glared at his wife.

"If something weird happens call me. What was that about?"

"I just don't want her to feel alone when her powers start coming in," she replied defensively.

"I thought we weren't going to mention anything about that?"

"I didn't. All I did was tell my daughter to call me."

Duante snorted and walked down the hall.

After Lanelle's parents left, she sat there, pouting, in the empty room. She was being forced to be a spy, and she hated it. She couldn't change it though. So while she was here she would be the best spy this school has ever seen.

Her pouting was interrupted by a knock at her door. Opening it, there was a girl smiling with her hand extended.

She had a light complexion and black curly hair. She was petite like Lanelle, but wore sneakers, jeans, and a t-shirt.

Lanelle, taken aback, shook the girl's hand.

"Hey, I'm Imani! I'm a sophomore here."

"Uh, hey Imani I'm-"

"You're Lanelle. I know. Your mom is kind of a legend around here, Janelle Sparks right?"

"She is?"

"Well, I just wanted to be the first to welcome you to Deceptive High." She winked, turned, and walked away.

Speeches

The professors and staff members visited the dorm rooms, telling all the freshmen to head to the cafe. Lanelle grabbed her folder and wondered if she should go down and meet Dion and walk with him. *Dion and Booker,* she thought.

She made it down the stairs and basically ran into Dion.

"Hey. We were just coming to look for you."

She fell in step with them, and they walked through the campus. She had no clue where she was going so she just followed the crowd. This place was huge. All around the campus there were old brick buildings, some smaller than others and some connected by enclosed bridges.

The cafe was filled with people mingling. Lanelle nervously rubbed her sweaty hands on her pants. She had decided in her room she was going to make the best of things, but she was feeling out of place.

A voice came over the loudspeaker. "Everyone go to the area that matches the color of your folders."

Lanelle and Dion stopped and looked around.

"I'm this way. Orange," Dion said pointing in one direction.

"Nope, I'm red," Booker said.

"And mine is blue," Lanelle sighed. "I'll catch you guys later."

Lanelle approached the area with the big blue circle hanging above it. There was a staff member in the middle of the group talking to the students. Lanelle squeezed into the circle so she could hear what was being said.

"Hello freshman! My name is Monica Michaelson and I am one of your Introduction teachers. Intro is a class that all freshmen are required to take along with their core classes needed for a high school diploma."

Monica was very animated when she spoke; her hands moved around constantly and she smiled a lot.

"So, that's like social studies, science, math and English. Think of Intro as your elective class. In this class, I will be teaching all different methods like: computer systems, combat fighting, surveillance techniques, counterintelligence, covert and overt operational styles."

Lanelle's folder said she was most likely good with covert operational styles and combat styles.

"The goal for this is to figure out where you guys excel and that's what path you will take here at Douglas."

Monica was looking around the group as she spoke. She spotted Lanelle and winked at her. Lanelle awkwardly smiled back and then shifted, not wanting to draw attention.

"So, right now we are going to go across campus to my classroom where we can speak more intimately, in a quieter environment. Follow me!"

* * *

Dion made his way to the orange section and squeezed in with the group circled around someone standing in the middle. Once he got a good spot, he realized it was that Jason dude from earlier.

"Hello all. My name is Jason Jetson, you can call me Mr. JJ. I am the Introductions teacher for you guys. Intro is a class where -."

Dion stopped listening and looked around the group. He was excited about this whole spy thing. But, he saw how hurt Lanelle was and couldn't throw his feelings in her face. There were some fine girls in this school. He smirked, knowing he would do great here.

Jason grabbed his attention again. "So, let's go over to my classroom and we will talk in more detail."

The group filled out to follow Jason.

"What's up," Dion heard from beside him. He turned and saw two people were talking to him.

"What's up, I'm Dion."

"I'm Quashawn and this is my sister Tariana. This thing blowing your mind too?"

Quashawn was a shade darker than Dion's caramel one. His hair was cut short with designs shaved into it. He was taller than Dion and a little more built. Tariana had micro braids in her hair that she had pulled back into a ponytail. She had a dark complexion and had a dressy style like Lanelle.

"My parents told us a few months ago, but I'm ready to get started. Y'all freaked out?" Dion responded.

"You got a brother?" Quashawn asked.

"Naw, I have a sister. She's my twin."

"Is she in this group?" Tariana asked enthusiastically.

"Naw, she's in the blue group. I can hook y'all up later though.

After all these speeches, y'all can follow me back to our dorm. We in Howard."

"I'm in Howard too," Tariana explained "but Qua is in Mitchell."

Dion kept talking to Quashawn as they approached another building. He liked the dude, thought he was cool. "We should exchange numbers," Dion handed Quashawn his phone.

Quashawn took the phone and added his number. When he was finished, he used Dion's phone to call himself and then handed Dion the phone back.

After the speeches, everyone was dismissed. Classes started in three days so they had the weekend to catch up and get settled in. Most of the freshmen arrived the previous Monday and spent the week here. Dion wanted to, but Lanelle didn't. They ended up coming today because it was the last day.

"What's your room number, Dion?" Tariana asked.

"Um, I'm not sure. I'm on the first floor in the middle, all the way back."

"Okay, once Qua comes over we will find you."

"Alright cool."

Dion began walking back in the direction of the cafe. From there, he knew how to get back to Howard. Once he got back to the café, he decided to look around.

They had an ice cream bar and the coffee bar was open. There was a big salad bar in the middle. The left side of the room had four different stations: Pizza, tacos, hamburgers/hot dogs, and chicken. The right side of the room offered Chinese food.

Dion walked over and got two coffees. Lanelle would kill him if he just got one for himself.

On his way back to Howard, Booker caught up with him and they walked back together.

"Where'd you get the coffee from?"

"They had it in the cafe. There is an ice cream bar open too."

"Aww, and you were so nice to get one for me too," Booker said in a sing-song tone.

Dion chuckled. "Naw, man. This is for Lanelle."

Lanelle. Booker liked Lanelle. Not only did she look good, but he liked her attitude, too. It was just his luck that she is his roommate's brother. He'd get to keep her close, well he had to keep her close.

"Speaking of Lanelle," Booker started cautiously. "What's up with her, anyway?"

Dion gave him the side eye. "Why, you feeling my her?"

"Naw, I'm just asking."

Dion scoffed. "Yeah, okay. Nothing is up with her. She's just taking this hard."

Booker stared off. "Oh, okay," he said, not wanting to say anything else to make Dion more suspicious.

Maybe this won't be so bad

Lanelle was sitting in her room, listening to music on her computer when her door busted open. She sat up and screeched. When she saw it was Dion, she put her hand to her chest in relief.

"You idiot, why would you do that? I just died." Lanelle noticed he wasn't alone. Besides Booker, he was with two other people.

He had a huge grin on his face. As if reading her mind, he said, "this is Tariana and Quashawn. They were in my orientation class." Dion turned and looked towards the people he'd invited into the room. "Get comfortable y'all."

Lanelle scowled at her brother and rolled her eyes. "Hey y'all I'm Lanelle. Yes, y'all can find a place to sit."

Lanelle's bed was big enough for Tariana, Dion, and Booker to sit on it with her. Quashawn pulled up her desk chair and sat next to the bed.

"So, what was in everyone's folder for a suspected area of interest?" Quashawn asked. "Mine was Protecting Services."

"What is that?" Tariana asked. "Like bodyguards and stuff?

I got that one too."

"Well, it can't be a bodyguard if you got it too." Quashawn said. Everyone laughed. Tariana reached over and punched him in the arm.

"Mine said Covert, that's all," Booker said.

"Mine said Covert and Protecting Services," Lanelle said.

"I got Cyber Surveillance," Dion said. "I'm smarter than all of y'all."

Lanelle sucked her teeth. "Whatever. They probably know all about how you cheated in Mr. Blinks' class last year."

"Dang girl, why you gotta tell my business like that?" Dion whined.

"It's just a sister thing. Tari does it to me all the time. They just talk too much."

"Oh, What. Ever," the girls said at the same time.

"See," Quashawn jokes, gesturing towards the girls.

"Anyway. I guess the classes go from –"

She was interrupted by a knock at the door. "Dang Lanelle, what other friends do you got besides me?" Dion asked. Lanelle threw a pillow at her brother and slid off the bed to go get the door.

Lanelle got up and walked towards the door. She stopped abruptly and blinked a few times. Everything was weird. The door was black, and she saw blue, orange, red and yellow colors swirling around.

Lanelle blinked and rubbed her eyes, when she opened them again everything was back to normal.

Hmm, that was weird, she thought.

When she opened the door, Imani was standing there with a wide grin on her face. "Hey girl!"

"Oh, hey Imani. Come in. Guys, this is Imani."

"I'm sorry, I didn't mean to interrupt."

"No sweat, the more the merrier right?" Dion added. He got off the bed and walked over to Imani. Making a big gesture, he held his hand out for hers and bowed. "I'm Dion. The better twin. Nice to meet you."

Lanelle rolled her eyes and bumped into Dion on the way back to her bed. The room laughed when he stumbled. Back on the bed, Tariana and Lanelle slid over to make room for Imani.

Everyone bombarded Imani with questions as soon as she got comfortable.

"How is it like here?"

"What do we do?"

"Which classes are you in?"

She laughed, holding up her hands. "Whoa, whoa. One at a time."

"Give us the goods," Dion prompted.

"So I live on the third floor. I have a roommate, Ayanna, we run in different circles though. They gave me Cyber Surveillance. I also take a Protection class as an elective."

"What's the difference? What do the classes mean?" Lanelle asked.

"I just started in Cyber Surveillance, but they are basically teaching me how to hack. I guess I was pretty good at computers. Protection classes teach you how to fight. There are different types of protection classes. Each one has a different teacher and a different fighting technique. If your specialty is something other than Protection, like me, you can choose to take extra classes for elective. If your specialty is Protection, you take all the fighting classes."

"So, in your Intro classes your specialty could change. They put what they think it is, based on what your parents say. But once you go through all the tests, you might have a different skill.”

Imani had everyone's attention. “Covert is basically a spy. You're out there in the field. Every Covert agent has to know all the Protection styles. If you're just Protection, that means you're basically a bodyguard. Usually, no one has just Overt Operations. Covert and Overt go hand in hand. An Agent has to know both. Covert agents take acting classes too.”

The group talked the entire night. They had a good time laughing and telling stories. The siblings embarrassed each other.

On the way back to their rooms Dion said, “Hey Booker, I noticed you were awfully quiet back there.”

“Yeah man, I don't know. I was just having a good time laughing at all of y'all.”

“Oh, okay.”

Dion didn't push it, but it made him think of Booker's childhood, whether it was bad or not.

They walked the rest of the room in silence. Booker was glad Dion didn't push things, but he knew he was suspicious. He didn't know how long he could keep his secret.

1st day of class

Dion and Booker headed out of the dorm. Dion had Math, which he hated. Booker's first class was Introductions.

Dion would much rather be going to Introductions than to Math.

Outside, there were staff members directing the student to their buildings. Dion and Booker's classes were in two different directions, so the friends went their separate ways.

Dion arrived at Math and smiled when he saw Imani sitting in the front row. He was relieved to see a seat behind her. There was no way he would sit in the front row of any class.

"Hey girl," he said, tapping her on the shoulder.

Imani turned around, scowling. Once she realized who had touched her, she grinned. "Oh, hey Dion. you're in this class?"

Dion held his hands up. "Dang girl! If looks could kill. I'd be dead." Dion dramatically fell back in his chair.

Imani giggled. "Sorry. I didn't know who was touching me."

Dion fixed himself in the desk and pulled his laptop out of his bag. "No sweat. Do you know this teacher?"

Imani averted her eyes. "I kind of took this class last year. I didn't do so well. Since we need core classes to get a traditional high school diploma, I have to take this class again."

"I'm pretty good with numbers. If you get stuck, I can help you out."

"I'm going to need it. They put me in Cyber Surveillance and I hate Math. I'm going to have to switch specialties if I don't get a handle on this."

"Hey Mani." Imani and Dion turned around and saw a girl coming towards them. Her long black hair brought out her caramel complexion. She wore faded jeans with a tank top with a jacket tied around her waist. She wore glasses that were hooked to a chain.

"Oh hey Ayanna, this is Dion. Dion, this is my roommate Ayanna."

Dion lifted his chin. "What's up?"

Ayanna smiled at Dion and then looked at Imani with a raised eyebrow. Imani looked back with a 'what' expression on her face. Ayanna sat in the back of the class.

"She failed, too?" Dion asked.

"No, she's a freshman. We know each other from back home in Mount Holly."

"Oh so you're close. We are from Charlotte, South Charlotte."

"Okay class. Welcome to the first day of Freshman Math." The teacher said as he wrote his name on the board. Then he turned to the class, clasping his hands together.

Imani's phone chimes and the teacher glares at her. She gave an apologetic look and took her phone out to silence it. Glancing at the screen, she saw a text from Ayanna.

Ayanna: Is that the legacy, did you plant the bugs already?

The teacher cleared his throat, and Imani jumped. She put her phone back in her purse and focused on what he was saying.

As he walked around giving group work, Dion leaned forward. "Want to be partners, or you going with your roommate?"

Imani had pulled her phone back out, texting Ayanna back quick.

Imani: He's a twin. His sister has the single room, so she was picked as the legacy I guess. I hung out with them last night.

Dion cleared his throat, and Imani jerked her head up. "Yes," she said.

"Who are you picking as your partner?"

"You said you would help me, are you changing your mind?"

"Naw but I thought you would want to pair with Ayanna."

Imani scoffed. "Yeah, like we don't see enough of each other already." Imani's phone buzzed. "Sorry, this is the last one. I really need to pass this class.

Ayanna: Do you have to plant the bugs on both of them?

Imani: idk they said 1st I would have to bug the legacy. But they're twins. Which one do I bug. They only gave me 1. ttyl I need to focus.

Imani looked at Dion and laughed nervously. "Okay, I'm all yours."

Dion rolled his eyes, looking unconvinced "Okay let's go."

* * *

Lanelle walked into her class and was relieved to see Booker and Tariana sitting next to each other. She sat in the seat next to Tariana, "Hey guys."

Tariana smiled. "I'm glad I have you guys in this class. I was worried."

"Me too girl."

The teacher walked in and introduced himself as Mr. Benjamin. "We will introduce you to multiple topics. You will take multiple tests. The point of this class is to find what you're good at. What skill should we focus on developing? Once you go into your specific program next year, I still recommend you choose elective to keep you well rounded," he explained.

The three of them sat in their seats eagerly listening. While the teacher was talking, he walked up and down the aisle. Lanelle found that weird.

"So he's one of the teachers who don't stay still?" she whispered to Tariana.

Tariana giggled, then pretended to cough as the teacher approached them. He walked through their aisle and when he passed Booker, he briefly squeezed his shoulder.

Lanelle raised her eyebrow and looked at Tariana. She, however, is paying her no attention. Instead, taking notes like she is supposed to be doing. *That was a 'I know you' touch*, she thought.

Filing it away for a future conversation, she took out her laptop and opened her One Note app. Making a folder for *Introductions*, she began listening and taking notes.

"Okay, your first assignment is a two-part assignment. In class you will have to get into teams. Each team should have one or two Covert Agents, one Cyber Security agent and one Protective Services agent. Once in your teams, I will give everyone a folder. You'll have one week to complete, assignment due at the end of day Friday."

Booker turned and looked at the girls. "So obviously we're on the same team, right? We just need a Cyber person to join us."

The three awkwardly looked around the room. Some people jumped right into groups, and others were milling around.

Tariana stood up. "Hey, we need a Cyber over here. Any takers?"

Lanelle covered her mouth with her hand to keep her laugh in. A girl walked up. "Hey. My name is Kasa. I am a Cyber." She had a copper skin tone with long brown hair that teased the top of her butt. She wore glasses and was dressed casually.

"Great, come sit. I'm Tariana, this is Lanelle and Booker."

Kasa smiled at Lanelle and Booker. Except she looked at Booker a little too long. Before Lanelle could give it any thought, the teacher came by and dropped a folder in front of them. It had *Mission* written in big, red letters. Lanelle grabbed the folder and opened it. The first paper read memo, she read it aloud.

"Today you have been given the task of finding the mole that is embedded in our classroom. Yes, that's right. We have a mole. Someone in the classroom who is not welcomed. I gave you all the information we have. It is your team's duty to find the mole and bring them to your leader (the teacher)."

"This is going to be cool," Booker enthused.

"Yeah, so cool." Kasa said, staring at Booker.

Why does she irritate me? Lanelle thought.

"Lanelle, what else is in there?" Tariana asked.

Lanelle looked through the folder and saw some emails, news clippings, and photos. She spread the items on the table in front of them right when the teacher walked up.

"Hello team number 4," he began. "Your mission is to find a mole in the classroom. There is someone in this class who is not supposed to be here. Pranks have been happening during orientation week and I have one more student than I am supposed to have on my roster. The other teachers and I got together and figured out that the mole is in this class. We don't know who it is, what they want, or where they came from. This group has until Friday to figure it out."

He paused, waiting for questions. "Good luck," he said after a few moments of silence, winked at Booker, and walked to the next group.

Lanelle looked around. *Am I the only one who saw the wink?* She thought.

"Okay, let's look at the pranks first," Booker reached over and grabbed the photos. One was of a statue with paint splattered on it. The second picture was of a bunch of electronics, ruined by water damage. The third picture was of the trashed café; tables and chairs turned over, condiments all over the floor. The final picture was of a computer.

"Here is a list." Lanelle said. "Prank number one was the defacing that statue. It's the one that is in the front of the grounds."

"Yeah, it is the founder of the school. It is really special around here. Every year, after the first week of classes, the whole freshmen class gets welcomed at the statue. It's like tradition," jumped in.

"How do you know that?" Lanelle questioned.

"I just looked it up," she responded as she waved her phone back and forth. "When I searched for the statue, the first link that popped up was on the welcoming event."

"So, that means someone knew the significance of the statue, especially the first week of school. I wonder how long it takes to clean that. I think I will have to find a janitor and ask them." Lanelle offered.

"I'll go with you," Booker volunteered.

"Okay," Lanelle said. "The next prank was when someone broke into the room that held the class sets of the gadgets that are used in the Freshmen classes. They poured water on everything, ruining them."

"So, we are looking for someone who can pick locks. Where

would we find someone who would know how to do that?" Kasa wondered.

"How do you know they picked the lock?" Lanelle asked.

"Well, the door was locked right?" Kasa shrugged.

"Right," Tariana jumped in. "So either they had the key, or they picked the lock. Kasa and I can find out who all had access to the key to that room. You and Booker should take the picking the lock angle."

"We can ask Imani. She is a Sophomore. She would know which kids pick locks." Lanelle offered.

"How do we know it's not a Freshman?" Kasa asked.

"It's just a guess. Why would Freshmen do pranks that sabotaged the Freshmen?" Lanelle said.

"What if it's not about the Freshmen class but about a specific teacher or staff member?"

"Okay, you two can run that angle. Find out if there is a staff member who does the welcoming thing and teaches the class that uses those gadgets."

"What are the last two pictures?" Booker asked.

This might actually be fun

"The third prank was completely trashing the cafe. According to this, it happened the same day we met there and broke into groups. It took the cleaning staff and volunteers all day to clean it in time." Lanelle read.

"So I got here at the beginning of orientation week. That cafe is open 24/7. But it only has staff members there until 8 p.m." Booker supplied.

"So Tariana and I should take that one. We can talk to the staff in the cafe, see what time they left, and what time the earliest person came in the morning. We would know our timeline then." Kasa supplied.

"Alright students, the class period is over. Remember this assignment is due Friday but from now on you have to work on it on your own time." The teacher announced.

"Booker, come here please," the teacher said. Lanelle glanced at him, skeptical.

"Meet me at my room after classes, okay?"

Booker looked nervous and a bit upset.

"Or we could meet in your room, or the cafe or something," she quickly added.

Booker glanced at her. "Oh, huh? Your room is fine. You should get going. Don't want to be late on your first day.

Booker stood there while Lanelle, Tariana and Kasa grabbed their things and walked out.

Booker huffed and went to the teacher's desk. "Yes," he sighed.

"How have you been settling in?"

"Dad, I thought we agreed on not doing this."

"Not doing what? We agreed that we wouldn't disclose to your peers that I am your father. How is it going with Dion?"

"Dad, I am not spying on him for you. Once I graduate, I am not even going into this stupid agency, I'm going to college and getting far away from you."

"Is that anyway to speak to your Father?"

Booker coughed. "Father? I was in foster care until a month ago. Or did you forget? I am going to be late for class. Can I go?"

Without waiting for an answer, Booker turned and walked out of the classroom.

Lanelle was standing at the door trying to listen. She did not hear much, except for Booker calling the teacher, Dad.

She scurried off before Booker came out and caught her.

Dad? She thought. *Why wouldn't he tell us his father worked here?*

Ready, set, go

Booker walked up to Lanelle's room and knocked on the door.

"Hey come in, I just got back. I'm almost ready."

Booker closed the door behind him and went to sit in her desk chair. "How were your classes?

"They were fine," she said, fumbling through her backpack, stuffing things into her fanny pack. "Core classes were normal, I have a lot of homework from them."

"Same here. Regular school stuff after the first class."

Lanelle stood up "I'm ready, where to first?"

"Let's walk through campus and find the statue and see what it looks like. Then we can go find a janitor."

"Okay, I'll text Imani and see if she can have dinner with us. We can ask her about lock pickers there."

The two walked through campus, orienting themselves. People were under the trees, laid out with blankets. Some people with headphones, others with books.

Some were playing catch and Frisbee. There were people gathered in groups and people hanging out solo. The statue was in the middle of the campus with yellow caution tape surrounding it. The head was clean and then as your eye went further down the paint got thicker and thicker.

"Dang, they only got the head clean. This isn't going to be ready for the end of the week."

Lanelle signed "No, it's not. This makes me think it's someone trying to sabotage Freshmen, not a teacher."

"Well, I don't know. What if Kasa was right? And there is one specific teacher who does all the Freshman stuff and the mole wants them to look bad?"

"How would the statue fit into that though?"

Booker thought for a moment. "It could look bad on that teacher if they were the only one to have to cancel the welcoming thing," he shrugged.

They sat down on a nearby bench. Lanelle took a picture of the statue with her phone. "I wonder when the statue was ruined and what type of paint that is, not coming off with a normal wash?"

"That's a good point. What type of paint doesn't come off with water?"

"We need to find a janitor. Is there like an office or break room?"

"I have no idea," Booker stood and stretched. "Let's just walk around and see what we can find."

"Good Idea."

* * *

"Hey, Kasa," Tariana yelled across the area dubbed The Square. It was where four buildings met with a big fountain that connected the four of them.

Kasa turned towards Tariana. "Oh, hey."

Tariana jogged over to catch up with Kasa. "I was just coming to your room. Is now a good time to visit the tech room, see what we can find?"

Kasa shifted nervously. "Um,"

"Oh, I'm sorry if you already have plans." Tariana added quickly.

"No, it's not that," Kasa replied quickly. She grabbed Tariana by the arm, pulling her closely.

"I was trying to play it cool," she began to whisper. "You see that group of guys over there, don't look obvious."

Tariana turned her head towards the group.

Kasa pulled on her arm "Tariana," she squealed. "I said don't look obvious."

Tariana giggled. "Yes, what about them?" She whispered

Kasa began to walk slowly, dragging Tariana along with her.

"Those are the native guys on campus."

Tariana looked confused. "Native?"

"Yeah. I'm Native American, Catawba."

"Ahh," Tariana said. "So, when you say Native, you mean other Native Americans?"

"Right, and that's Delslin. The one with the short hair and the blue jeans."

Tariana was about to scoff about the 'blue jeans' description. Until she looked over and out of the group of six guys, only one had on blue jeans.

"He's cute," Tariana replied.

"Cute? He's the hottest boy in this school."

Drool was threatening to flood Kasa. Tariana decided to take things into her own hands. "Delslin," she called. The whole group looked towards her and Kasa's cheeks turned so red it was almost like she was a cartoon.

She waved at them and Delslin started walking towards them. Another one followed like he wouldn't miss this for the world.

"Hey," Delslin said. "I'm Delslin, this is my brother Jacy." He pointed his thumb behind him.

"My name is Tariana, and this is my friend Kasa." Tariana moved slightly. Kasa was directly behind her.

"So what's up? You called me," Delslin asked.

"We were just wondering if you guys wanted to go to the cafe with us today?"

Delslin smirked. "Yeah, sure," he replied.

"Great, six o'clock?"

"Yeah, that's cool. Both of you right?"

Tariana was stifling a laugh at Kasa, so she didn't hear him. "Hmm?"

"Both of you will be there, Kasa too?"

Tariana elbowed her. "Yea-uh-yes. Both of us. I mean. I'll be there too."

Delslin grinned. "Good."

As the boys walked away, Kasa put the back of her hand to her forehead dramatically.

"What is wrong with you woman?"

"Now you have a dinner date with Delslin and I get to be with his cute brother."

Flustered, Kasa changed the subject. "Where are we supposed to be headed? To that classroom right?"

"Ha!" Tariana screamed. "Yes, let's go to the classroom."

Done

Dion lay across the bed in his room. He decided to get a start on all the homework he had. But about an hour into doing homework, he didn't feel like doing it anymore. So he put his headphones in and turned on his music.

His phone chimes with a text message and he picks it up.

Imani: Hey! Are you in your room? I need help!

Dion debated whether he should answer or not. Imani was fine and he wanted to spend all the time he could with her. He didn't want to do math though. He was over doing homework, period.

Who was he kidding.

Dion: Yeah, I'm here. Come down.

There was an instant knock. "Dang," Dion said as he rose and headed to the door.

"Hey," Imani said cheerfully.

"You got there fast," he said, motioning for her to come in.

She giggled a little bit. "Sorry, I was sort of waiting outside the door."

"Yeah, I got that," he mumbled.

Imani stood in the room, looking awkwardly at the bed, then to the desk, and back again.

"You can spread your things out on the bed," Dion suggested.

Imani let out a breath she didn't know she was holding.

Hmm, Dion thought, *she's really anxious.*

"Okay, let's see what you got," Dion said, flopping down on the bed next to her.

The next hour went by quickly. Dion helped Imani with the part of the homework he had already done and they had worked together to finish the part he hadn't completed yet.

She was right when she said she struggled. She got the hang of it after a while, but needed someone there working it out beside her.

When Dion was done, he put his books and computer to the side and laid back on his bed, groaning loudly.

"Nothing like homework to make you want dinner. Want to go eat?"

Imani shifted her gaze around the room. "Uh, I actually was going to eat with Ayanna. You can come if you want."

Dion noticed her hesitation. "Nope, I can catch up with Booker and Lanelle. You go eat with your roommate."

Imani smiled awkwardly and went to gather her things. Her jerky movements caused some of her supplies to fall on the ground. She mumbled, "Sorry," and got off the bed to pick them up.

After a moment she popped up, "Okay, I'll see you later."

"Okay–" Dion said, but before he could finish she was at the door.

* * *

Imani closed Dion's bedroom door and took a deep breath. She pulled out her phone and sent a text.

Imani: Done

She slipped the phone back in her pocket and walked off.

Ayanna was in their room with Move Together by James Bay playing on repeat. Imani rushed into the room, dropping her things by the door.

Quickly, she unplugged the portable speakers.

Ayanna bolted upright. "Hey!"

Imani flopped down on her bed. "I did it."

"Did what," Ayanna huffed.

"The bug, I did it."

Ayanna sat up straight, her eyes wide. "How, where, who," She stumbled.

"I went down to Dion's room for help with math."

Ayanna lifted one eyebrow, "You were in his room, was his roommate there?"

"What?" Imani asked. She shook her head. "No, it was just him."

"And what were you doing alone in Dion's room?"

"I told you I needed help with math. Ayanna, stay focused."

"Okay," Ayanna said, rolling her eyes. "What happened?

"I dropped my stuff off the bed and then stuck it underneath. I was so scared. I'm pretty sure he thought I was a nutcase."

"So did you let them know you did it?"

Imani guiltily looked over at her bag. "I sent the text, but I haven't checked my phone since.

"Well, go get it!" Ayanna exclaimed.

Imani took a deep breath and dug through her bag for her phone. When she was sitting back on the bed, she slid her phone over to Ayanna. "You check," she mumbled.

Ayanna hurriedly grabbed her phone and put in the code Imani shared with her.

"It says '*where is the device located*'?"

"Text back: in Dion's room," Imani said.

Once the text was sent the girls sat there staring, waiting for the three dots to pop up.

The phone dinged.

"Why didn't you put it in the other one's room," Ayanna read. "Wait, there's another one 'forget it, this will have to do. I will send your next task in a few days."

Imani put her palms over her face. "I thought I was done after that," she said in a muffled voice.

Ayanna pulled Imani into her and rubbed her back as she cried.

Hmm?

Tariana and Kasa walked into the Cafe. It had been the first time Tariana had been in there when everything was open and running.

"They have Chinese food!" she squealed.

The girls walked over and stood in line. Kasa looked around the Cafe. "They are not coming," she sighed, disappointed.

"Give them a minute," Tariana exclaimed.

Kasa mumbled and kept looking around. When the girls reached the buffet line, she sighed again.

Once through the line, Kasa spotted Booker and Lanelle. "Hey, there's Booker and Lanelle, can we go sit with them."

"We can," Tariana said, waving at Lanelle. "Or we can go sit with Delslin and Jacy," she pointed to Delslin. He was at a back table, waving his hand to get their attention.

Kasa swore under her breath and Tariana laughed, pulling her towards the table.

Kasa sighed in relief when she realized Delslin and Jacy were on the same side of the table. The girls settled in.

Tariana thought Jacy was cute. He was taller than Quashawn with long hair that was pulled back but not in a ponytail.

"So you said your name is what?" He asked.

She giggled with a mouthful of food. "Tariana," she said

muffled.

He chuckled. "Sorry,"

"No, that was rude of me to dig in without properly introducing myself. Jacy right?"

"Yeah, it's Jacy. So what brings you to Deceptive High, as they call it?"

Tariana rolled her eyes. "My parents. We kind of didn't have a choice, but I've gotten used to the idea. I think it's cool now."

"We knew all along," Jacy began. "The whole spy thing isn't something our parents kept secret."

Delslin jumped in. "Yeah, we always knew. It was kind of cool as a kid. Knowing every time out parents went out they were going, like, undercover. What about you, Kasa?"

Kasa blushed when Delslin said her name. "I, uh, my mom told me when I was young. My father isn't in the picture. My mother decided to live off the Res, that's the reservation where we stayed," she explained, looking at Tariana. "I don't know why, but my father had a choice of staying with my mother or staying on the Res. He chose to stay. "

"Dang, that sucks, I'm sorry," Tariana said, while rubbing her arm.

Kasa shook her head. "No, I'm good. Anyway, my mother told me where she was going when she left me with my nanny, Jessica."

"Do you guys plan on staying in the Academy after graduation?" Delslin asked.

Tariana shrugged. "I don't know. I guess I'll have to wait and see."

"I want to follow in my mother's footsteps, so I'm staying," Kasa said. "What about you two?"

"I want to stay, Delslin doesn't," Jacy shrugged. "But who

knows, we could change our minds, either one of us."

"Not likely," Delslin mumbled.

"What do you want to do?" Kasa asked Delslin.

He averted his eyes "Uh, I want to go to college. Like normal college to be a Veterinarian.

Kasa's and Tariana's eyes got wide.

"That's so cool," Kasa replied.

"Yeah, that's dope," Tarianna chimed in. "I guess my dream would be," she trailed off.

"Don't leave us in suspense now," Jacy said smiling.

Tariana looked down at her plate. "Well, I want to be a master stylist. Like, all types of hair, nails, massages. And I want to have my own business where it's like a one stop shop for all beauty needs." She looked up hesitantly to see what their reactions would be.

Kasa raised her hand "first customer, right here!"

Tarianna giggled in relief.

Delslin and Kasa, Tariana and Jacy broke off into separate conversations. Tariana discovered that Jacy liked riding horses, all types of music except rock, and riding dirt bikes.

Jacy learned Tariana liked to sing, do arts & crafts, DIY projects and she also liked to read.

Kasa couldn't form one full sentence without stumbling and stuttering. Which embarrassed her and caused her to stumble more. Delslin told her about his record collection. She found it fascinating that he had old time records of artists that were around today. Not just 50 years ago. Delslin loved movies and he could play the piano and guitar. He even offered her lessons.

Kasa told him that she liked to write poetry and short stories. She liked music but didn't know how to play anything. She liked all kinds, besides rock and roll.

When they had finished eating, Delslin asked, "Can I have your number?" He handed his phone over to Kasa. She smiled and took the phone, recording her number.

"Jacy is going to walk me to my room, okay?" Tariana said to Kasa.

"Wait, we never worked on the project." Kasa exclaimed.

"I have homework. I'll come to your room after, okay?" Tariana said, giving Kasa a 'just agree' look.

"You can tell me about your project, maybe I can help," Delslin offered.

"Yes," Tariana jumped in. "Sounds good, I'll stop by after I'm done."

"Okay, see you later," Kasa finally said.

Kasa watched Tariana and Jacy walk off. Her hands were clammy when she grabbed her phone after hearing it buzz. She looked at her screen. *'**Relax, be yourself and bag the hottie,**'* said the text from Tariana. Kasa smiled and looked at Delslin.

"So, in our introductions class," she began.

* * *

Lanelle and Booker furrowed their brows in confusion when Tariana waved and went to another table during dinner.

"I wonder what's up with that," Booker said.

Lanelle looked around until she saw where Tariana and Kasa had gone to and smiled. "Oh, I'm sure they have a good reason."

Booker followed her gaze. "Oh," he replied dryly.

Lanelle focused on eating her food. She wanted to ask him about Mr. Benjamin, but she didn't know how to bring it up.

"Umm, so –"

"What type of paint did the janitor say was used?" He asked, cutting her off.

"They said it was regular spray paint," Lanelle answered. "They were using water and rags to wash it off when they needed to be using something oil based. That's why it took so long."

"So it really isn't that big of a sabotage then? Didn't the janitors say they aren't cleaning it on purpose?"

"Yeah, they don't want it to happen again before the welcoming ceremony, so they are going to wait to clean it until the night before."

"Too bad they don't have any clue who did it," Booker said with a mouth full of food.

Lanelle took a deep breath and tried again. "So, umm, you seemed pretty friendly with Mr. Benjamin. You've met him before?"

Booker froze. "What do you mean friendly?" he asked, slightly defensive.

"Nothing bad," she rushed out. "Just it seemed like you knew him."

"Why are you trying to make something out of nothing?" Booker shot out.

Lanelle's eyes widened. "Whoa, I didn't mean anything bad. I was just asking. Why are you getting defensive? If you haven't just say no." Lanelle had her napkin in her hand. Suddenly, she screeched and dropped it on the table. Both Lanelle and Booker looked at the napkin on the table. Well, what was left of the napkin.

"What the heck?" Booker said, barely above a whisper. "How did you do that?"

The napkin was black and crumbled. Booker reached over and patted it a few times to put the fire out.

"You burned the napkin," he said.

Lanelle sat there, in shock. She didn't know what happened. One minute, she was holding the napkin. Then, she was getting irritated with Booker. The next thing she knew, something was burning her hand.

Booker touched her arm. "Lanelle, how did you do that?"

"I didn't do anything," she proclaimed.

"Hey guys," Imani yelled from the other side of the Café and waved at them. Lanelle waved and turned towards Booker. "Are you going to tell her?"

Lanelle was blinking rapidly and her eyes were beginning to water. He assumed she was trying to stop herself from crying. He'd seen girls do that before.

"Tell her what? We need to figure out who picks locks right?"

Lanelle exhaled. "Right."

Imani came over and sat down. It seemed like she'd been crying. She tried to cover it with elaborate eye makeup but her eyes were red.

"So what's up? You guys wanted to talk to me?" she asked.

Lanelle hesitated and Booker spoke up "What do you know about lock picking?"

Imani's eyebrow shot up. "That's a third-year class."

"Wait," Booker laughed. "Lock picking is a class?"

"Yeah, that's what you mean right?"

Booker smiled. "Maybe this school isn't half bad," he mumbled, then raised his voice again. "But, we have a project and we need to know who is good at picking a lock. Where would we go to find someone like that?"

Imani thought as she chewed her food. "Hmm," she said finally "Well, I know that lock picking is a third-year class. So I would assume anyone who was good at it would be either a third or fourth year. As to specifically who, I'm not sure." She frowned and shrugged. "Sorry."

"No, that's cool. Thanks for the info." Booker looked over at Lanelle, who was still zoned out. They ate and made small talk, but Imani kept eyeing Lanelle suspiciously. Booker had grabbed the napkin and slid it in his pocket.

"You know there's a trash can right?" Imani said.

"Well you know," Booker shrugged.

Imani giggled. "Must be a guy thing," she replied.

Conflicted and confused

Booker was in the bathroom, preparing to take a shower. He couldn't stop thinking about Lanelle burning that napkin. He didn't care what she said, she burned it. With her hands.

How else could she have done it? Was she hiding a lighter in her hand or something?

When Booker's father had come to him and said he made sure he got Dion as a roommate and asked Booker to look out for him, Booker thought about it.

He hadn't spoken to, or even knew who his dad was, his whole life. He felt kind of honored that Derek (Mr. Benjamin) trusted him with something like this.

The more he thought about it, the more upset he became. Especially since it seemed like the only way he could see or talk to Derek is when he wanted to talk about "his mission", that's what he kept calling it.

He didn't want to be a father, at least not Booker's father. He just needed him to find out whatever it was he was after about Dion.

Plus, Dion and Lanelle were good people. He liked them, especially Lanelle. He didn't want to cause any trouble with Dion that would get in the way of him getting to know her better.

But that napkin.

That's one thing he couldn't let go. He would have to ask her about it again. She looked scared. Or was she panicking because she had just shown him her trick. He just couldn't tell. Booker got out the shower just as confused as he went in.

* * *

Lanelle was pacing back and forth in her room. She was confused, scared, and worried about Booker.

First, her parents tell her they are spies. Then she is going to a spy boarding school. She has an episode where she basically can see through the walls and the door, even if it was in weird colors, and now she set a napkin on fire, with her hands!

Lanelle went to her bed and grabbed her phone. Her mother picked up on the second ring.

Janelle: Hello, how's everything going Lanelle?

Lanelle: Mother, I set a napkin on fire!

Janelle was quiet for a long time. Lanelle heard shuffling in the background and then her father's voice came on the line.

Duante: Hey Lanelle.

Lanelle: What is going on, what's happening to me?

Janelle: Lanelle, when I was at Douglas I was top of my class.

Lanelle: Right, I know. What does that have to do with me?

Janelle: If you would just be quiet and listen. Some of the others scored top five, but no one's scores were as high as mine. I had some help becoming so good. Your father and I knew that either you or Dion would inherit the same kind of help that I got.

Lanelle: Mother, what are you talking about?

Duante: Lanelle, your mother can also set things on fire, she has thermal vision, she has more strength and speed than the average person. She can command the wind and put up a protective barrier to stop things from harming her. You will be able to do some of these things too.

Lanelle staggered over to her bed and sat down. She couldn't believe what she was hearing.

Lanelle: So on top of everything else, I'm Wonder Woman?!

Janelle: I will come visit you this weekend and we can talk about it in person. But, Lanelle. You cannot let anyone, especially the staff and instructors, know that you have these abilities. I will come and teach you how to control them. Right now, your abilities are connected to your emotions. You need to stay calm.

Lanelle: So, we're Wonder Women?

Janelle: Yes, dear. We ARE Wonder Women.

Lanelle: My life just can't get any worse, huh?

Duante: It's not as bad as it seems right now, Lanelle.

Lanelle: Um, I got some homework to do. I will talk to you guys later.

Lanelle wanted to hang up before they could keep talking, but she knew better. Knowing her mother would call back and yell at her for being rude, she sent a text, *'please give me some time'* and hoped her mother would let this one slide.

Pool Days

The next few days were a blur. Between classes and this whole magic thing, Lanelle was exhausted and ready for the weekend. The welcome ceremony was the next night after dinner hours and her parents would be there in two days.

Out of all the things her father had told her she could do, she only was able to do the fire thing again. She didn't have to be holding the object to set it on fire. She had to admit it was kind of cool.

It was awkward between her and Booker. They went on like nothing had happened, but she felt the tension just beneath the surface. Their project was due tomorrow Booker, Tariana, Kasa, and herself knew who did all the pranks. They had a couple of theories on why, but had one more day before they had to pick one.

Even though things were awkward with Booker, they were progressing too. Every time they were together, he held her hand. She wasn't sure if he knew it or not, it seemed like an automatic response kind of thing, and she didn't complain.

Dion joked a few times, but Booker didn't let go. They just laughed and shrugged it off. After the whole fire thing Lanelle thought Booker would run for the hills. If she were in his shoes, she would.

Lanelle walked across campus to the pool. She always loved swimming and had been good at it. She was fast and agile in the water, and now she knew why. A boy approached her when she was making a couple laps.

"Hey," he shouted.

Lanelle stilled and looked up to see who was calling her. "Yeah?" she called back.

"I'm Jalen, Captain of the swim team. I've seen you a couple times coming here and you're good. You wanna' join the team?"

Lanelle swa a bit closer to the edge of the pool so she didn't have to shout. "Is this team any good? Do you compete?" she fired at him.

"We are third in our division. We could really use a good swimmer like you to take us all the way."

Lanelle stared at him, unconvinced.

'Okay, listen," he said, as he pulled a piece of paper out of his pocket. "I wrote my number on here. We have an interest meeting next week. Think about it and come to the meeting. Then let me know what you are thinking."

Jalen walked over to where Lanelle had her phone and other belongings and dropped the piece of paper. He turned back to look at her and waved before he walked off.

Lanelle never thought about being on a team though. She promised herself she would make the best of her time there. What would be the harm in joining the swim team?

"I thought you were supposed to be swimming!" Dion shouted, interrupting her thoughts.

Lanelle rolled her eyes. "I am swimming."

Dion, Booker, and Quashawn came up to the edge of the pool. "Well, look little sis. Swimming is this thing where you move your arms and legs and that makes you move through the water. But, you actually have to be moving your arms and legs to move."

Lanelle sucked her teeth and splashed up water. All four of them gasped in surprise.

Dion raised his hands to protect his face and the water froze in mid air, leaving an icicle design.

"What the hell," Dion exclaimed as he moved around the icicle examining it. Lanelle raised herself up on the edge of the pool and slowly touched the icicle. The spot she touched glowed orange and then the ice turned back into water and splashed to the ground.

"So you both can do it," Booker said breathlessly.

"What. The. Hell." Quashawn and Booker said at the same time.

"But I didn't freeze it," Lanelle said, looking at Booker.

"So, he can freeze and you can make fire. That's dope."

Dion's head jerked up. "Wait, fire, what about fire?"

"Hey y'all," Tariana yelled. She was walking over with Kasa and Imani in tow. There were two boys behind them.

Lanelle looked over to Dion with wide eyes "There are many here, not in front of everyone," she pleaded. Lanelle touched the rest of the ice cicles and the water fell to the ground.

"What's the issue?" Imani said as they approached. "I can feel the tension."

Dion walked over to Imani. "So, this happened," he said as he put his arm around her grinning.

Imani blushed and playfully pushed him away.

"Well. we all know Booker and Lanelle are together," Tariana began.

"Hold on," Lanelle interrupted.

"Despite what they say," Tariana giggled over Lanelle. "This is Jacy," pointing to the boy behind her. "And Delslin," pointing to the boy behind Kasa.

The two brothers smiled and lifted their heads in a nod.

"What was going on when we first came up?" Imani asked.

Lanelle splashed in the water and floated backward. "So we are not here to swim?"

Quashawn pulled his shirt over his head and jumped in the water. The rest of the boys followed. Tariana, Kasa, and Jacy went over to where they saw Lanelle's things and carefully took off their cover ups. Imani stood there for a moment, still suspicious. "Are you coming?" Dion asked from in the pool.

* * *

"Okay, I'm wrinkly. Time to go." Lanelle swam towards the edge of the pool.

"It's got to be time to eat by now," Booker said, following her.

Once everyone was out of the pool, they made plans to meet at the cafe.

"Uh, I'll see you guys back at the room later. I already have plans." Quashawn said.

"So, your girlfriend can't meet us?" Tariana asked.

Quashawn sucked his teeth. "Shut up, Tari."

"So, it is a girl you don't want us to meet!" she mocked.

"I never said that, shut up. I got to go. I'll catch y'all later." Without waiting from her to respond, he turned and jogged for the door.

"He does this all the time. We never figure out who his girlfriend is until I go snooping around," she giggled.

The group walked out of the pool area. The girls bunched up in the front talking and giggling. The boys followed behind them silently.

Pieces of the puzzle

Lanelle was sitting on her bed when Dion came barging through the door. Lanelle shrieked. "Don't you knock!"

"We have a lot to talk about," he announced, sitting next to her. "Tell me about the fire."

Lanelle put her books down and crossed her legs under her. "Has anything weird been happening to you?"

"No, we are not making this about me. You have some explaining to do."

Lanelle's eyes got wide. "Me?" she exclaimed. "You froze the water. It turned into ice. So who has explaining to do?"

Dion sighed heavily. "Okay, so we both need to be having this conversation. It sounds like you've been talking to Booker about it."

Lanelle smirked and crossed her arms. "You jealous?"

"Psh, naw I ain't jealous. I'm just wondering why you would tell him and not me?"

"I didn't tell him," Lanelle said. She explained about the encounter in the cafeteria and what she had learned talking to their parents.

"Dang," he said, deep in thought. Lanelle stared at him for a few long moments. She was just about to break the ice when his head jerked up. making her jump slightly.

"So we on some Black Lightning type stuff" he grinned.

Lanelle took a deep breath and relaxed. "Well, when you start electrocuting things, you better tell me," she rolled her eyes.

"Right, like you told me about the fire," he shot back.

Lanelle sucked her teeth. "Sorry, okay," she said.

Dion stared at her for a moment. "Uhh, what? Why are you being weird?" Lanelle asked.

"So, we doing a movie, or what?" he said.

Lanelle grinned and grabbed her laptop.

* * *

Dion and Lanelle hung out the whole week, trying to make their powers work, deciding to keep it to themselves, and figuring out how to control it. Dion, after some practice, discovered that he could freeze more than just water. He could stop any object from moving, except people. He tried to stop Lanelle and although she felt it in her body, she was able to fight it.

"Ya know, Imani has been asking me all week about what she missed in the pool."

Lanelle looked at him. "Really, isn't that weird that she won't let it go?"

"I don't think it's weird. It definitely is irritating though."

"Well what do you tell her?"

"I just say I don't know what she is talking about. I wish she'd just drop it."

"Well have you told her to drop it?"

Dion signed and got up. "Tomorrow, we will meet in your room. You have more space."

"I told you we need to do it in my room." She crowed happily.

"Yeah, yeah, yeah, whatever."

Dion was walking to the gym after dropping Lanelle at the pool for a swim team meeting. His specialty was listed as Cyber Surveillance, but he wanted to learn Combat too. In the evenings, some of the Combat professors held classes where they helped train whoever showed up. He had been going all week and loved it. *No way does Lanelle get to be the only bad ass,* he thought.

At the gym. Dion headed straight to the locker room. He rounded a corner and then slowed when he saw Booker. As he was about to call out, he noticed that Booker was arguing with someone. Dion hesitated there for a moment, then walked one section of the lockers behind him so he could eavesdrop.

"I told you, I am not going to be your puppet," Booker said, fists clenched at his sides.

"We had a deal," the older man said. Dion didn't know him, but he had seen him around campus. "The only reason you are here is to get close to them. Figure out what's so special about that family."

"I will not spy on them. I don't care what beef you had with their parents back in the day. Leave me out of it."

"Pssh, beef? You make it sound like one of your mediocre problems with one of your little friends. This is bigger than some beef."

The door opened and a few voices filled the locker room. Dion hurried around the locked and filed in after the group of guys who just walked in. "Hey Book," Dion said, lifting his chin slightly when they made eye contact. Dion looked at the man and said, "Hello, uh, Sir."

Mr. Benjamin chuckled. "Hello son, I am Mr. Benjamin. Booker's dad," he said as he stuck his hand out.

Dion returned the handshake. "I'm Dion."

"Oh I know who you are," Mr. Benjamin bellowed. "You're a legacy, the Sparks' boy."

Dion smiled politely. Mr. Benjamin placed his hand on Booker's shoulder and squeezed before leaving.

"Dang bruh, I didn't know your father worked here." Dion said as he walked towards the lockers.

Booker followed him. "Yeah," he mumbled. "I don't want people knowing."

"Oh, aiight, cool," Dion said as he dropped his pants and stuffed them into his locker.

"Well, I'm going to go to the track. They have an meeting today."

That caught Dion's attention. "What do you run?"

"I did pole vaulting last year. I hear they have a team here."

"That's what's up. I didn't know you were into that."

Booker smiled awkwardly and saluted before leaving.

Dion finished stuffing things in his locker as he watched Booker walk away.

Wash Day

Imani was in Tracie and Tiffany's room, two seniors who lived on the top floor of Howard. She sat crossed-legged as Tracie braided her hair. She was braiding it half way and left Imani's natural curls out in the back.

"So," Tracie said, while smacking on some gum. "You know they say you're dating that Freshman legacy, that true?"

Imani bit on her lower lip. "Uh, yeah. Dion, we're talking."

"You know his parents cheated while they went here right?" Tiffany jumped in. She was laying on her bed, scrolling through Social Media.

"Cheated, how does anyone cheat?" Imani asked. curious.

Tiffany shrugged. "She's right though," Tracie jumped in. "Everyone knows. They were too good to not have cheated. Our dad said he wouldn't let those two legacies, your man and his sister, make it through cheating like their parents did."

Imani tightened her fists in her lap to prevent herself from fidgeting. "Well, I don't know anything about that."

Tracie took her hair and pulled her head to the side. Imani looked up at Tracie, who was looking down at her in disbelief. "You telling me you ain't heard nothing from him about how his parents cheated?"

Imani looked away and shrugged. "We don't really talk about

his parents."

Tracie continued braiding. "Well, next time take a break with whatever yall be doing and ask him."

Imani blushed, but stayed quiet. Tiffany started talking about what the shade room posted on Twitter and the conversation went away from Imani and Dion.

They cheated, she thought. *How did they cheat? Hell, how did anyone cheat here? That must be why Monica told her to plant the bug in Dion's room. They think that the twins have whatever their parents had that made them so good.* She didn't know which of the twins were cheating. What she did know, was that she didn't want to be in the middle anymore.

"Well, let all your little friends know that we do hair for a homework assignment per style," Tracie said, still smacking that gum, as Imani handed them the essay she'd typed.

"Yeah, and don't forget to ask your boyfriend, shit, we wanna know."

"Thanks," Imani said, purposefully not agreeing and walked out the room. She checked her phone when she was walking down the hall. She was afraid to check while she was in there. She didn't want Tracie or Tiffany thinking it was Dion. She had a few texts from Ayanna and this girl she was doing a project with in one of her classes. She didn't have any from Dion and decided to text him.

Imani: Where are you?

He hadn't responded by the time she made it to the level his room was on. She left the Howard building and texted Ayanna.

Imani: Hey, I just finished getting my hair done.

Ayanna: Girl, Let me tell you! You remember Delslin and them right? The natives?

Imani: Yeah what's up?

Ayanna: Well he is dating Kasa, that one that hangs with Lanelle and them.

Imani: He was never yours to begin with Ayanna

Ayanna: I'm dying, can you come back to the room?

Imani: omw

Imani put her phone in her back pocket and chuckled.

When she got back to her room, Ayanna barely let her close the door before she started talking.

"Can you believe this? I mean what am I going to do?"

Imani put her bags down and went over to sit on her bed. "Ayanna, am I missing something? Did you tell him you liked him and didn't tell me?"

Ayanna's eyes got wide. "No," she exclaimed. "That would be so embarrassing. What am I supposed to do, walk up to him and go 'uh, hey Del my name is Ayanna and I'm feeling you?'" she said with a low voice.

Imani giggled. "Well, first of all, I am pretty sure he doesn't sound like that."

Ayanna sucked her teeth. "And second," Imani continued. "If he doesn't know you like him, you can't be mad he is talking to someone else."

Ayanna signed dramatically and flopped backwards on her bed. "How about that guy from your English class?" Imani asked.

"Do not try to change the subject. Wait, you mean Mike?" Ayanna grinned wide. "Yeah, he is fine!"

Imani laughed. "Yeah, and he is feeling you."

"No he isn't," Ayanna countered.

"If you weren't so busy daydreaming about Delslin, you would have noticed the way he stares at you in class."

Imani's phone buzzed and she leaned over the bed to grab it. It was a text from Dion.

Dion: Just got back from the gym. Where are you?

Imani: In my room. You coming over?

Dion: Yeah, wait for me to shower.

Ayanna sucked her teeth. "Let me guess, I have to find somewhere else to sleep tonight?"

"What?" Imani said, looking at her.

"Was that Dion? He is coming over isn't he?"

"Yeah, we are watching a movie. You can watch one with us." she said as she got up.

Ayanna rolled her eyes. "Yeah, I'll pass," she said dryly.

* * *

Lanelle walked back to her room with a towel wrapped around her head.

"Dang, are you done yet? You've gone to the bathroom to wash your hair like three times." Booker said, when she closed the door.

"I had to wash the conditioner out," she whined. "Wash day is no fun for me either Booker."

"We have mad homework. I thought this would be quick."

"You see this hair," Imani asked, pointing at her wild, thick afro.

"Yeah, since you mentioned it. Are you going to straighten that or something?"

Lanelle picked up her spray bottle and threw it at him, hitting him in the head. "Ahh, what was that for!"

Lanelle stood with her hands on her hips. "What's wrong

with my hair like this Booker?"

Rubbing his head Booker, peeked up at her. "Nothing, I mean. I was just asking what else you're going to do with it."

Lanelle squinted her eyes. 'Well. I was going to twist it out, but now I think I'll rock my 'fro for a few days."

Booker looked around the room, trying to avoid eye contact. "'Aight cool," he mumbled.

Lanelle turned towards her mirror and looked at her wet poof. Circling her hands together, she created a ball of heat. She raised her hands and put her head in between her hands. After a few moments, she dropped her hands.

"You just dried your hair?" Booker asked in astonishment.

Lanelle cursed herself. She shouldn't have done that in front of Booker. She turned around, jumping when Booker was standing right behind her. He reached up and touched her hair. Lanelle leaned back and drew her eyebrows together. "I know you didn't just touch my hair," she demanded.

"There was no fire this time," Booker said, ignoring her as he went up to touch it again.

Lanelle grabbed his hand midair. "So you're going to touch it again!" Before he could respond, there was a knock at her door. Lanelle rolled her eyes and went to open it.

"Oh, Mr. Benjamin, Hi. Booker is here, come on in."

"Hello you two," Mr. Benjamin bellowed. "What's this about no fire?" he asked, eyeing Booker. Mr. Benjamin walked over and made himself comfortable on the bed, crossing one leg over the other.

Lanelle frowned. "How long were you standing at the door?"

"Oh, don't worry," Mr. Benjamin chuckled. "I wasn't eavesdropping."

Lanelle turned her mouth down and furrowed her brows. *But*

you just said what we said, that means you heard us. Which means you were eavesdropping.

"We were talking about her hair being set on fire," Booker responded.

Lanelle's head darted to Booker, her eyes wide.

"All that stuff she puts in it before she dries it, isn't that stuff flammable?" He asked, turning towards Lanelle.

Lanelle rolled her eyes and sucked her teeth. *Good save*, she thought. Booker's eyes went wide. She gave him a quizzical look. "You just said that in my head," he mouthed to her.

Lanelle's eyes got wide.

"Uhh, everything okay over here?" Mr. Benjamin asked, missing the exchange.

"Yeah, fine," Lanelle and Booker said at the same time.

Mr. Benjamin raised one eyebrow and looked back and forth between the two.

"So ah, what are you doing here?" Booker asked.

Mr. Benjamin stared between them a few more times and then cleared his throat. "I just wanted to check up on you that's all," he said, putting a hand on Booker's shoulder.

Booker cringed and fought not to pull away. "Well, I'm fine," he responded curtly.

Mr. Benjamin let his hand drop, smiling widely.

"How else can we help you?" Lanelle asked timidly.

"I know you're not trying to rush me away from my son."

Lanelle's eyes got wide. "I'm sorry, I didn't," she began to stutter. "I no longer want you in my room, can you please leave?"

Mr. Benjamin sneered. "You think you can stop me from seeing my son?"

"He can leave too," she replied, taking a step back.

"What!" Booker exclaimed. He turned to Mr. Benjamin. "Get out of here. You always mess everything up. What are you even doing here?"

"Naw son, I want to know who this little *legacy* thinks she is. Telling me to leave." His eyes were focused on Lanelle. He took a menacing step forward. Lanelle's back bumped against the wall. Her hands curled into fists at her side. "Please, just leave my room."

"You think you can just kick me out, huh?" Mr. Benjamin said.

Lanelle felt so small. He was towering over her. *How did he go from so nice to scary*, she thought.

"Okay, time for you to go," Booker said as he ushered Mr. Benjamin towards the door.

They're watching you

"What was that all about?" Lanelle said, as she turned back towards the mirror to finish her hair. Booker closed the door. "Make sure he actually leaves. He was listening at my door before."

Booker sighed, reopened it and looked down the hall. "He's gone," he said as he stalked back over to Lanelle.

"What is the deal with him anyways?"

"No, no," Booker interrupted. "We are talking about how you said something in my head."

Lanelle shrugged her shoulders. "I didn't mean to."

"How long have you known about the mind reading thought thing?"

"I didn't know until you gave me that weird look. It's new to me."

"Well, do it again," Booker pressed.

Lanelle separated her hair into quadrants and she was untangling the first section. She walked over to her dresser and grabbed a bottle, squirting some in her hand as she walked back over to the mirror.

"Lanelle," Booker whined.

Lanelle huffed and dropped her arms. Turning around towards Booker she thought, *I wish you would let me finish my hair.*

"Did you hear that?" she asked annoyed.

Booker sighed. "Come on, you have to do it right."

Lanelle narrowed her eyes and put her hands on her hips.

"I heard that," Booker said.

"Heard what, I didn't say anything.," Lanelle said, eyes getting wide. "Wait, you mean you heard my thoughts? I did it again?"

* * *

Dion and Quashawn walked to the cafe from class. Dion was admiring all the people lounging on the grass and benches. He said, "Want to throw the ball around after we eat? Come out here and chill?"

Quashawn looked around and saw a bunch of girls, upper-classmen, laying out in the sun in their bathing suits. His eye twinkled as he grinned.

"Hell yea," he said. "Isn't that Imani?"

Dion followed where Quashawn's head was nodding towards. Past the group of girls, Dion saw Imani talking to someone.

The two were on the lawn near the library. It had three columns out front, just like all the other buildings. "Imani and Mr. JJ," the two said together.

"She looks pressed," Quashawn said.

Dion slowly kicked his foot on a big boulder that lined the main walkways and watched the interaction underneath the columns.

Imani and Mr. JJ were obviously arguing. Dion began walking again, this time across the lawn towards Imani and Mr. JJ. "Hey, what's up?" He said, when he got within earshot.

Imani glanced casually and then looked back at Mr. JJ who

didn't pay Dion any attention. Imani whipped her head back around and looked at Dion with bulging eyes. "Dion, what's up?"

"Conversation looks tense," he said.

Mr. JJ glared at Imani and then looked at Dion. "Not everything's your business, *Legacy*." He sneered and then stalked off.

Dion furrowed his eyebrows.

"Damn, well hello to you too," Quashawn mumbled.

"What was that about?" Dion asked.

"Let's just go, where were you two headed?" Imani asked as she grabbed his arm, afraid to meet his gaze.

Dion lifted his arm out of her reach, refusing to let her tug him along. "What was that about?" He asked again, eyes narrowed as he looked at her.

Imani shifted from foot to foot. "Dion please, can we just go?" Biting on her lower lip, she looked at Quashawn with pleading eyes.

"Uh, I'm going to hit you later Dion. Bye 'mani," Quashawn said, lifting his head slightly in a nod as he walked away.

Dion stared at Imani for a few more moments, eyes piercing. She thought she saw, what, hurt? Whatever it was, was gone before she could pin it down. He turned and walked away.

"Dion , wait," she said, calling after him. Jogging to catch up to him, she placed a hand on his bicep. Her shoulders deflated when he flinched.

"Is he messing with you, hurting you?" Dion asked, not looking down at her.

"No," she screeched. "It's nothing like that. OMG Dion."

"What am I supposed to think then?" He glared at her. "I don't like lies and secrets. I am just getting over my parents -"

"I am nothing like them, this is a different situation." Imani interrupted.

Dion softened his gaze slightly. Imani averted her eyes. Dion jerked his arm and began walking again.

Imani sighed heavily, quickly grabbing his hand, and squeezed when he tried to pull it back. "Come this way. Please," she said.

Dion sucked his teeth and followed her to the middle of the yard where the benches were. "Please sit," she said.

Dion sat down and looked around at the people lounging with books and playing music on their phones. Some were out doing homework or just laying down enjoying the weather. He watched as people walked down the pathways to one building or another. He hated that his day was ruined by whatever she had going on. He wanted to be carefree and enjoy the weather too. But he had a feeling whatever she was going to say was going to piss him off.

He stared at her. Imani took a deep breath. "There is a listening device in your room." She said in a rush, cringing.

His head jerked back "What, how do you know that?"

"Because I put it there," she said softly.

Dion slid over on the bench, putting more space between Imani and himself. His jaw was clenched so tight she saw the muscles jumping.

"And why would you do that?" He asked coolly.

Avoiding eye contact Imani continued. "Everyone thinks you and Lanelle have some secret advantage. I guess your parents kicked ass when they were here and after, when they joined the Academy. People always thought they cheated somehow. So Mr. JJ asked me to bug your room and try to find out what the Sparks secret is."

Dion nodded his head slowly, digesting what he just heard. After a few moments, he stood up. Imani jumped up and reached for him. "Please, don't," she pleaded.

Dion looked at her, eyes glistening. The next second his eyes went cold, void of emotion.

"So you got close to me and my sister, just to what? Figure out if we have a secret." He sucked his teeth and sighed. Imani looked at him, tears falling. "That was then," she pleaded. "It's not like that now."

Dion rolled his eyes. "I'm not about to sit here and do no movie scene or nothing." The people around them were looking at them curiously. "I'll catch you around."

Dion turned and walked away.

"Dion please," she pleaded.

Dion turned around and looked at her. "You might not want to stand here crying and shit. Won't want the staff knowing you told the secret."

The second before he turned around, she saw his eyes glisten.

Can you believe this?

D ion swung Lanelle's door open, causing her to jump and squeal.

"Dang, you never knock," she complained, holding her hand over her heart.

"Guess what Imani just told me?" he replied.

Lanelle sat on her bed and crossed her legs. Dion sat down next to her and told her what Imani told him.

"So people know about Mom's advantage," she stuttered, her anxiety rising.

"Naw, they were jealous that her and Dad were so good. They didn't *know* anything." He emphasized.

"But they thought they knew enough to have Imani get close to us in order to spy on us. Did you find the bug and who else is spying on us?

"Booker said he knew someone who had one of the things to search for it."

"What are you going to say to Imani when you calm down?"

Dion frowned at her. "What do you mean? I'm not going to say anything to her. Period." Grabbing his phone, he began swiping aimlessly.

"What, you're just going to stop talking to her? Did she apologize?" Lanelle leaned forward, trying to look him in the eye.

"Who cares," Dion yelled, causing Lanelle to jump back "She lied, she was sneaking around and was never down for us."

Dion jumped up, and started pacing back and forth in front of the bed.

"She *is* down for us, she told you didn't she? She made a mistake, Dion."

Dion turned towards her, hands in a wide gesture. "So why did it take so long for her to tell me?"

"Look how you're acting," she made a hand gesture towards him. "I wouldn't have wanted to tell you either."

Dion narrowed his eyes. "Why aren't you freaking out? We both should be acting like this."

"It's a big deal obviously. But she agreed before she even knew us. She apologized. I just don't think we should cancel her."

Dion stared at her, dumbfounded. "I can't believe you're taking her side." Dion paced up and down her room again.

"I'm not taking sides, I am just trying to stop you from making these decisions when you're mad."

Lanelle didn't believe he would respond. Dion got like that sometimes, being so mad he just couldn't talk to anyone.

Lanelle reached over to grab her phone. He would talk to her when he was ready. Plus, she wanted to talk to Imani.

Lanelle: Hey girl

Imani: I can't believe you're still talking to me

Lanelle: Why did you do it?

Imani: I didn't have any reason not to at the time. Please don't hate me

Lanelle: I know you made a mistake

Imani: yes, and I regret it. That's what I was arguing with Mr. JJ about. I was telling him I couldn't do it anymore. That they needed to leave me alone.

Lanelle: They?

"You know, Mom and Dad lied to us," Dion mumbled. Lanelle dropped her phone, sitting back up on her bed.

"That hurt me too," she replied softly.

Dion sucked his teeth and rolled his eyes. "I didn't say I was hurt, it just pissed me off."

Lanelle moved on the bed so she was closer to her brother.

"And Imani made you feel the same way hur-er , pissed off."

She said it as more of a statement than a question, but he nodded anyway. Dion draped his arm around her. "I guess it's just me and you now."

Lanelle hugged him back. "Uhh, you mean, you, me, and Booker. My boyfriend didn't do anything."

Dion began chuckling and playfully pushed her back on the bed.

The Adventure, Adventure

The crew was sitting out on the lawn. Booker leaned against a tree with Lanelle laying underneath his arm. Tariana and Quashawn were laying on an old, tattered yellow and green quilt. Dion was laying on a beach towel with a picture of a guy with shades on the front. Lanelle had her phone, playing 'Today's Hip Hop' Spotify playlists.

There weren't a lot of people out. The sun was setting, causing the sky to begin to change colors and a cool breeze caused some leaves to tumble past them.

Tariana noticed Imani approaching "There you are!" she exclaimed, breaking the calm and peaceful atmosphere. "It's been like a week, where have you been?"

Imani smiled sheepishly and held up a flyer. "Well, there's the 'The Adventure, Adventure' competition coming up this weekend and they are accepting teams of six."

"Whatever that is," Quashawn began. "We're in." He jumped up to grab the flyer.

Imani's eyes flickered towards Lanelle, who smiled and waved. She waved back, releasing a breath she didn't know she was holding and then looked at Dion. He was staring at Quashawn and she averted her eyes. Her shoulders slumped, disappointed.

"It's like a scavenger hunt through the woods behind campus. We need to do this. Sign us up Imani." Qua said before returning to his spot next to Tariana.

"Is that okay with everyone?" Imani asked tentatively.

Dion grunted and Lanelle kicked him. "Yeah, we're in Imani." Lanelle said.

Dion glared at her.

A group of girls walked up to them. One of them, Sasha, swung her waist long braids back and forth and they landed swooped to one side of her head. "Hey Dion," she cooed. "We need a sixth member for our Adventure team, you in?"

"Oh, so you're going to completely ignore everyone else sitting here?" Lanelle snapped.

Sasha looked at her and rolled her eyes. Fixing her gaze back on Dion. "Well?" she prompted, pouting and batting her eyes.

"The nerve," Lanelle said at the same time as Tariana and Imani sucked their teeth.

Dion looked up, noticing they were the girls who he and Quashawn watched lounging last week when the whole Imani thing happened.

Lanelle sat up and tilted her head, looking at Dion. Dion rolled his eyes at his sister and glanced at Imani quickly before looking back towards Sasha. "Sorry," he said. with a crooked smile. "I have a team."

Sasha pouted again, poking her bottom lip out. "But they already have a Legacy. We want one too."

Imani stiffened and Lanelle whipped her head around to look at Sasha.

"I'm sure you can find another Legacy." Dion said, smoothly cutting off Lanelle.

Sasha opened her mouth to protest again when Tariana cut

her off. "He said no, DANG!"

Sasha narrowed her eyes and glared at Tariana. "Just come on Sasha," one of her friends said. Sasha made a show of lingering on Dion and then turning slowly to walk away. Imani was glaring at Sasha's back when Lanelle said, "So what do we have to do?"

Imani sat down in the midst of everyone. "Well after we sign up they give us the clues. At midnight the game starts and we have to race to get to the trophy first. I didn't get a chance to do it last year and Ayanna already has a team." She lowered her eyes. "Or I wouldn't have asked."

"What do you mean you wouldn't have asked, you leaving us for Ayanna and 'em?" Tariana asked playfully.

Imani looked uncomfortable but relieved that the twins hadn't told everyone what went down between them.

"So tell us about it," Lanelle said.

Imani smiled her thanks at the redirection and read the flyer to the group.

"That sounds fun," Tariana said.

"So are we all in?" Imani asked apprehensively. She looked around at everyone and her eyes landed on Dion. He averted his gaze and got kicked by Lanelle again.

Dion grunted. "Yeah, we are all in."

Imani smiled.

* * *

"Have I ever told you guys that I hate the dark?" Tariana whined.

Quashawn sighed. "For the 10th time since we left Lanelle's room."

Lanelle shoved Quashawn. "Girl, it's okay. It'll be fun. The first clue said 'somewhere high somewhere low. You'll start at the famous pole.'

"Yeah, and that is a flagpole. It is on top of the hill behind campus and during the night time they lower it," Imani rushed out.

As the crew worked their way through the brush behind one of the older buildings on campus, Tariana's head jerked at every crunch and rustle of leaves. The trees lined a well worn walking path.

Quashawn and Dion ducked their heads under some of the low hanging branches to get through some of the spots. Everyone had to walk single file; Dion led the way, followed by Imani. Lanelle was behind Tariana with Booker behind her and Quashawn bringing up the rear.

"Relax," Lanelle whispered in Tariana's ear. "It will be fine."

Tariana scoffed and Lanelle giggled. Lanelle looked down at her hands and wiggled her fingers, bringing a ball of fire to life. As soon as the flame illuminated. she closed her fist, putting it out. *What are you thinking?* She scowled to herself. Wrapped up in her thoughts, she hadn't noticed everyone in front of her stopped walking until she crashed into Tariana, causing both girls to fall.

The guys began laughing, with Dion howling the loudest. The two picked themselves off the ground, flinging dirt, leaves, and small sticks off their clothes.

"Look guys, the flagpole," Imani said in between giggles.

Happy for a distraction, Lanelle looked at the pole, but didn't see an envelope stuck to it. "If this is the right place, where is the next clue?

The rules said phones had to be left in their rooms. Lanelle and Dion had smart watches, but they were completely out of range out here.

"I guess we have to look around. I'm sure this is the place," Imani confirmed.

"Great, more crawling in the mud," Tariana grumbled.

Dion chuckled again and Imani elbowed him in the side. "Just come on," she said stifling her own laugh. Dion looked at her, hurt still filling his eyes. With one blink, all emotion was gone and he turned his head.

At the flagpole, the flag was low to the ground and tied off. They spread out, kicking leaves and dirt over in search for the envelope.

It's so dark, Lanelle thought. She stared down at her hands. *If only I could –*

Her thoughts got caught off by someone screeching. When she turned around, Quashawn and Dion were doubled over in laughter and Tariana on the ground. Lanelle held up her palm and pushed out slightly, causing Dion and Quashawn to stumble backward and fall.

Dion instantly glared at Lanelle. Booker was laughing so hard he was on the ground.

Why would you do that, leave her alone. Lanelle sent the thought to Dion. Her anger quickly dissipated when she saw the confused look on Quashawn's face. Her eyes were wide. She glanced at Imani who had her hand over her mouth, covering her laugh; and then to Booker who was still on the ground laughing.

So Dion and Quashawn are the only ones who heard it, she thought to herself.

Quashawn rose and began wiping off his clothes. Dion rushed over to Lanelle. "What the hell?"

"I meant that for you, but Quashawn heard it too. I don't

know how to control it yet."

"You can, what makes people hear your thoughts?" Dion sighed heavily. "Why do you get all the cool shit?"

"We need to call Mom and Dad."

Dion growled. "Yeah, I know."

"Here is the envelope," Tariana yelled as she held up the small black envelope. "This is what I tripped on that made me fall," she glared at her brother. "Not you."

Everyone crowded around as she tore the envelope open. **"Good job on finding the first clue. If your envelope is black, you are the first ones. To keep your lead, you need to go to the spot where it all started. No matter your year, you all started here,"** she read aloud.

They will not beat me

"Well," Tariana started. "I don't know what this means but what I do know is that we can figure it out anywhere but here, in the woods, in the dark."

"What is the place where it all started, do they mean our time here?" Lanelle asked.

"Yeah, who was here since the first day of orientation? Lanelle and I showed up later in the week."

Imani stood next to Dion and had to stifle a gasp when he didn't move away from her, for the first time that night. "I showed up late to my orientation too," Imani added.

"Well, I was here before everyone else because of my dad," Booker shrugged. "So I really don't know either."

The group turned and looked at Tariana and Quashawn.

"This is something we can talk about anywhere but here, in the woods, in the dark," Tariana repeated.

Quashawn pondered for a moment. "We stopped at a table that was at the gates and they gave us our building assignments. The next place we went was there."

Tariana heard something crunch in the woods next to her, jumped and squealed. She nearly jumped into her brother's arms.

"For real, let's get out of here. There is something in these woods.”

Quashawn grumbled. “Yeah, us.”

Lanelle glared at Quashawn. “You two suck as brothers. Come on, we will go to the gate. We are in first place anyways. We will lose our lead standing here.”

“Thank God,” Tariana mumbled as they got back into their single file line and made their way through the woods.

Lanelle wanted to let Booker know what happened. But she knew she really needed to work these things out with her mother. She needed to learn how to control herself.

There was a loud crunch in the woods. Tariana and Lanelle whipped their heads.

Tariana whimpered. “I hate the dark y’all.”

“No,” Lanelle slowly said. “I heard it too.”

Quashawn sighed. “Do not egg her on Lanelle.”

“No, I heard something too.”

* * *

“Dammit Jason, be quiet!” Monica hissed.

“How am I supposed to know which stick to step on and which one to avoid? This is stupid, why are we following those stupid kids around?”

“We need to see what makes them special. There is no way I am letting Duante and Janelle win the Careers Award. Me, you, Benjamin. Any one of us deserves that besides them. Janelle always wins and I know she has an edge. If I have to go through her kids to figure it out, then I will.”

“I know, I know, but I am sick of sneaking behind these kids. Isn’t that what Booker and Imani are for?” Jason grumbled as he trucked back through the woods.

"Booker is being difficult. Benjamin says he actually likes the little brat and isn't playing ball. How is it going with Imani?" Monica asked.

"I haven't heard from her all week," he mumbled.

"So, if the kids are not working, then we will have to step in. We have a few months before they give that award and I will not let Janelle beat me."

***

They walked through campus, heading to the front gates.

"It's weird that no one is outside. Seeing everything empty." Lanelle commented.

"It's 1 am dummy," Dion replied. "Everyone is sleeping."

Lanelle narrowed her eyes. Dion gave her a warning glare. Lanelle scrunched up her face and rolled her eyes.

Booker grabbed her hand, winding his fingers in her. "What was that about, Brother sister stuff?"

Lanelle glanced around at their friends and slowed down slightly. Once everyone was a safe distance in front of them she leaned over and whispered, "I tried to send a mind message to Dion when we were back in the woods, and I ended up sending it to Dion and Quashawn."

Booker's eyes got wide. "What were you thinking? What did Quashawn do? How could you be so careless?"

"Chill, alright! I know I made a mistake. I thought I could control it enough to choose who I wanted to send it to. Quashawn just looked confused, that's all."

"You should go see your mom this weekend," Booker suggested.

Lanelle sighed. "I know. That's what Dion and I said. It's

time for a trip home. We haven't spoken to my parents, not really, since they told me."

"Come on love birds," Tariana shouted.

Lanelle rolled her eyes and grinned. "Shut up," she mocked as she picked up her pace.

Up ahead, were large brick walls with iron gates between them. The gates had a black box in the middle with a buzzer and a ID card slot. It is set up that everyone has to get out of their car either to swipe in or ring the buzzer and talk to the guards. It enabled the cameras to scan the visitor and the license plate on the back of the car. On either side of the black box were two large emblems with the letters DH on them. The thick trees on either side of the gate wrapped around until it reached two of the buildings on either side of campus.

"How do we get out?" Tariana asked Imani.

"Well, when I am in a car it automatically opens. I guess there is a censor. I am not sure on foot, I have never tried to get out by walking before." She responded, shrugging her shoulders.

"So there must be a sensor," Lanelle said. They began looking around the ground, stepping seeing if something happened.

"Guys," Dion began. "You think people don't sneak off campus. There has to be some way through without going through the gate."

Dion looked at the trees that lined either side of the gate. As he stared at the leaves, branches and the trunks all disappeared and all he saw was the chain linked fence that wrapped the front of the campus. About 50 yards from the front of the gate, there was a hole. Dion grinned. He was about to tell everyone about the hole and then hesitated.

"What's up?" Lanelle asked. "You look weird."

Dion grabbed her hand and brought her in the direction of

the hole. "There is an opening over here. Help me find it."

Lanelle scrunched her face up. "How am I going to help you find something you seem to already know where it is?"

Dion lowered his voice. "I saw through the bushes. There is a fence hidden behind the trees and a hole in the fence."

"You saw past the trees!" Lanelle squealed. Dion shushed her and she lowered her voice "That's dope. I can't do that."

"Stop making it so obvious and start looking around." Dion demanded.

You all started here

"Thank God you guys found a fence." Tariana said as the crew made their way through the hole.

"Let's look for an envelope or something out here," Dion said. When everyone split up, Dion focused as he scanned the area slowly. He grunted in frustration when he could not see the envelope. His vision had pulled back the trees and brush. It had even stripped the clothes off everyone, leaving them looking like blue and black objects with only their phones visible in their pocket.

What it didn't do is let him see the envelope.

"What's up?" Imani said, elbowing him playfully.

Startled, Dion jumped. "Dang girl, don't sneak up on me like that."

Imani grinned.

Dion's lips curved and then fell.

"Look," Imani began. "I'm sorry Dion, really."

"I know," he said softly.

Lanelle looked at Dion and Imani. She was glad her brother was giving Imani a chance.

She was kind of jealous that Dion could see through things. Scrunching up her eyebrows and nose, she concentrated on what was around her. Trying to pull back the layers just like

Dion said he did.

Stomping her feet she grunted, balling her fists. All she saw were squirrels and birds. Taking a deep breath she squinted, determined to make it work.

A black glove slapped on her mouth as a large arm wrapped around her stomach and pulled her backwards. It happened so fast she didn't scream.

Don't cry, don't cry she thought over and over again. A mantra in her head.

She kept her arms still at her sides. Her feet barely touched the ground. She fought to keep her toes down.

"You need to pay more attention," a raspy voice said.

Okay, it's a woman. I think. I don't know. Don't panic. Lanelle stops.

"You can get out of this, Legacy," the voice hissed.

Lanelle took deep breaths. *This person wants me to use my magic.*

Lanelle mumbled against the hand over her mouth. "Please, just tell me what you want."

The person gripped her tighter. Lanelle whimpered as the hand over her stomach pushed and pulled violently.

"Yo, Lanelle, we found it. Where are you?" She heard Dion shout.

"Dion, please stay away," she tried to yell. But her shouts were muffled.

The voice chuckled. "Your move."

* * *

Dion looked around. "Lanelle," he called again. His jaw ticked when she didn't reply. Everyone had gathered around to read the next clue.

Something didn't sit right. Where was she at? Dion called out one more time. "Nell?"

When she still didn't answer, Dion squinted his eyes and concentrated. Scanning the area around him, he pulled back the layers. Seeing the black figures outlined in blue of the squirrels and birds. The trees with the trunks and branches reduced to shadows and lines. He cursed when he spotted two people.

He couldn't make out what was going on. The entangled shadows made it hard to separate the lines.

Dion began walking towards the two shadows. He thought he heard whimpering. Was it Lanelle, was she hurt?

His pace picked up. He struggled to keep his concentration, he was getting scared.

As he got close, the shadows moved. Stopping, he followed the shadows further into the trees.

"Let's see if he continues to follow us, shall we?"

Dion's head jerked. Who was that? The voice raspy, but how did he hear it? Muffled whimpers caught his attention. That has to be Lanelle. But something didn't sit right.

"Lanelle, are you in here?" he called out. "We found the envelope, quit playing, and come on."

Waiting a few more moments, it took everything Dion had to turn around and walk back to the group. Something was up, but he had a feeling in his gut that going to help Lanelle would only make it worse.

"Hey, there you are. Where's Lanelle? The final clue is sending us to the pool." Imani asked when Dion came out of the trees.

Dion forced a shrug. "I think she's playing around or something." He forced himself to relax when he felt his teeth grinding.

Imani's eyes were filled with concern. He didn't trust her though. He couldn't trust her. She was against time. She had been this whole time. All that stuff about forgiveness Lanelle was talking about is bullshit. Thinking about Lanelle made his bones itch to run back and get his sister. She was in trouble.

Imani's gasp broke him from his thoughts. Dion whirled around and relief flooded him when Lanelle came out from the trees.

"Girl, you trying to scare us or something?" Imani asked with a mock attitude, hands on her hips.

"Nah girl, I was just looking. I didn't know you already found it," she replied hesitantly.

Imani's eyebrow raised and she stared at her. The suspicion behind her eyes were gone the moment later. "We have to go to the pool. That's where the next clue is."

Imani began walking away and Dion turned towards Lanelle.

"What the hell?" he barked.

"Someone grabbed me," she hissed. "The voice was all messed up. I don't know who it was and I couldn't get away. But they said -"

"Well, well, well, what do we have here." Lanelle was interrupted by Sasha and her team. "Team Legacy found our clue for us. Thanks guys!" she mocked as she snatched the envelope from Tariana's hand.

"So, you're going to give that back to me. Because if I have to come get it from you, I swear."

Sasha scowled. "Girl please. You swear what?"

They didn't have time for this. Dion wanted this whole game to be over as quick as possible. He needed to finish his conversation with Lanelle.

"Now Ma'," Dion struggled to remember her name. He smirked as he walked over to her. "You're about to do us like that are you?"

"I tried to get you on our team Dion," Sasha exhaled and tilted her head.

Dion licked his lips and smiled. Reaching his hand out, he brushed his hand over hers before setting on the envelope. "What if I said please?"

Sasha squealed and jerked her hand back. The movement startled Dion and the envelope fell to the ground.

"You burned me," Sasha said, rubbing her hand. "I like it."

Dion smiled and held up the envelope. "Thanks for this, we've got a race to win."

He turned and glared at Lanelle. Booker held on to her hands tightly.

You burned her?!

"**Y**ou burned her?" Dion accused them as they walked across campus.

Lanelle huffed. We have better things to talk about. Like um, I don't know, I was just kidnapped!"

"Don't be dramatic," Dion hissed. "What if her hand caught fire? Thank God Booker stopped you. Why are you being so reckless?"

Lanelle looked at him, her brows furrowed. The corners of her mouth turned down and she squinted. "Why are you so worried about her?"

Dion's eyes bulged. "Don't turn this around on me!" he nearly shouted.

"Your priorities are always busted."

Tariana twirled in a circle. "Come on guys. Quit the sibling rivalry until tomorrow."

Lanelle quickened her pace to catch up to the group. "What does the clue say anyway?" she asked.

"You made it back to the beginning, good job. Your next step is to dive in deep," Quashawn recited in an announcer voice.

Tariana chuckled and sucked her teeth.

"Oh okay," Dion said, needing catching up.

He walked over to Imani and put his arm around her shoulders.

She melted into him immediately, almost falling over when he went rigid and pulled away.

"Sorry, habit," he mumbled.

"Not a habit I want you to stop," she mumbled.

It took so long for Dion to respond, she thought he wouldn't respond.

"It is going to take me some time," he whispered.

Before Imani could respond, the door to the pool locker room slammed open. Everyone's head snapped towards the door, stopping in their tracks.

"What was that?" Imani asked. She trembled and grabbed onto Dion's arm .

No one spoke for a few long moments. They stared at the door waiting for something or someone to come out.

"So we got ghosts," Quashawn said, trying to lighten the tension.

"Y'all should go ahead and see what that was," Imani said, gesturing to Booker, Quashawn, and Dion.

Dion stepped forward. Tariana whined. "Oh no, I will not be left out here in the open. What if something happens?"

Quashawn whistled. "Stop being so dramatic."

Quashawn started to walk towards the door, followed by Booker and Dion.

Tariana began to follow. "Not leaving me out here," she mumbled.

Lanelle grabbed Imani's hand. "Come on, we might as well go."

Imani followed her, clasping her hands to stop the trembling.

As Dion approached the door, he tried to concentrate but he couldn't see through the building. The shadows danced with the blue lines and he saw everything that was in the walls. The electrical and plumbing. He cursed under his breath.

They were feet away from the door when they heard what sounded like footsteps.

Dion rushed forward and peered inside the door.

"What's up?" Quashawn whispered.

"I heard something, someone running in here."

Lanelle made her way to Dion. "What's everyone looking at?" she said too loudly.

"Shh," Dion hissed "I heard someone run through here." Dion stared at her, hoping she got the signal in his gaze.

"Guys, this is dumb," Lanelle began. "There is no one in here. Let's go get the other clue."

* * *

The hallway looked different at night. None of the lights were on and everyone's shoes squeaked at them as they walked down the hall. The light at the end of the hallway flickered. Lanelle could feel the weight of everyone behind her. It was like they were all on her shoulders, pushing her along.

She walked forward, focusing her gaze as she entered. instantly she saw everything in oranges, yellows, purple and reds. Everything that wasn't giving off any heat was a deep blue.

Someone was here. She saw footprints leading down the hall and into the locker rooms. She was going to tell everyone to check the locker rooms, but then she thought back to the person who held her in the trees.

They were waiting for her and Dion to do something. It's like they knew about the magic and was just waiting for them to prove them right. She couldn't risk her or Dion, so she passed the locker room door and headed straight to the pool.

Suddenly there was a slam behind them. She gasped while Imani and Tariana screamed simultaneously. Everyone spun around looking towards the sound.

"It's just the door closing," Quashawn said.

"By itself?" Tariana questioned.

"Well, it opened by itself didn't it?" he shrugged.

Lanelle's vision returned to normal. Taking a deep breath, she forced herself to focus. She had orange and yellow footprints leading to the door.

Someone was in here she thought, wishing she had enough control over her powers to talk directly to Dion without everyone else hearing her.

"It's nothing," she said instead. "Come on guys." Lanelle turned around and walked towards the pool.

The pool door slammed causing Tariana and Imani to jump and scream again.

Quashawn laughed.

Tariana glared at him. Imani puts her hands on her hips. "Don't be so childish," she said to him.

Lanelle turned towards Dion, grinning at the two girls. "Hey Dion, come here."

She puts her hand on his arm. "There was someone out there. I saw footprints right after the door slammed," she whispered.

"I was going to ask you to see if you could see through the walls when we were outside. I could only see in between the walls."

"I think someone has been following us," she said suddenly.

The two of them walked to the opposite side of the pool, out of earshot. Dion put his arm around Lanelle's shoulder. "What happened in the woods?"

"Someone grabbed me. It was weird though. They just

wanted to see me use my magic."'

"Wait," Dion interrupted. "They knew about your magic?"

Lanelle took a step back so she could look at him. "Not exactly, but they were waiting for me to do something. They knew I could get out. Plus, when you showed up, they dragged me further in. Like they wanted you to come." Lanelle huffed "Dion, I think we need to take Imani seriously. We really need to go home this weekend."

"Yea I know." Dion mumbled.

Long overdue

"I am so proud of you!" Janelle beamed. She was standing in the Master Bathroom, moisturizing her natural curls. "We won Adventure, Adventure two years in a row. I bet if we would've played our last two years, we would have gotten it all four years."

Janelle spotted Lanelle in the mirror and she sighed.

Lanelle sat on the bed picking at her nails. "Lanelle," she said in a stern voice. Lanelle looked up at her mother through the mirror.

"What have I always taught you?"

Lanelle sighed. "Say what's on your mind. You'll regret not speaking out more than you will with people's hurt feelings."

"Exactly," Janelle said as she went over to the bed.

Lanelle went back to picking her nails until Janelle cleared her throat.

"Mother, you set us up. We thought we were only there for High School. Then you put this spy thing on us, then this magic I didn't ask for. Our friends are spying on us. I have people kidnapping me in the woods," she shrugged. "It's just too much."

"God never puts more on us than we could bare," Janelle said calmly.

Lanelle jerked off the bed. "I'm not trying to hear all that right now!" she yelled.

"You can be frustrated and upset, that does not give you a pass on your behaviors. Sit back down and watch who you're talking to." Janelle said sternly.

Lanelle played with her fingers before sulking back over to the bed.

"Tell me about what happened during the game," she commanded.

Lanelle explained how Tariana was afraid of the dark, but she swore she heard something too. She went through when someone grabbed her. Janelle made her go through every detail, twice. She talked about their new powers, the door slamming, and the footprints.

"The footprints made me a positive Mother. Someone was following us."

Janelle clenched her hands so hard that blood dripped from where the nails were pressed into her palm.

Lanelle noticed the droplets of blood. "Mother," she exclaimed. Janelle closed her eyes, taking a few calming breaths. When she opened them, she unraveled her hand, and Lanelle watched in awe as her mother's hand healed.

"Can I do that too?" she asked, sounding more excited then she had since she arrived.

Janelle took her index finger and guided Lanelle's chin so that she was looking at her.

"We have to get some training in before you and your brother leave." A smile spread across Janelle's face. "We are so blessed this gift has touched both of you, but we have left you unprepared and that's on us. We cannot send you back unprepared."

Lanelle sighed, closing her fingers into fists. "See that's the thing. I wasn't unprepared. I mean I don't have any combat skills yet but I could have burned the mess out of them."

Lanelle giggled when Janelle gave her a knowing look. "Don't get too comfortable now," she warned.

"Mother, I didn't even curse,' she defended with a glint in her eye.

Janelle chuckled. "Yeah, yeah, yeah." She stood up. "Come on here, let's go get your brother so we can talk about these gifts.

* * *

"It's weird Ma," Dion sat on the arm of the chair. The family had gathered in the living room. The table was moved out of the center of the room and all the furniture pushed back to the edges, leaving a big space in the middle.

"It doesn't seem like Lanelle and my sight are the same. She can see through and tell if there are on the other side. I can't do that."

"Yes," Janelle said. She had changed into yoga pants, a grey t-shirt, and sneakers. "Lanelle has thermal vision. You pick up the heat signatures in living things and they come to you in oranges and yellows."

Stretching her left arm over the right side of her body, she pushed on her left elbow. "And Dion, yours is called X-ray vision. You can see through items and people. But if something is in between you and what you want to see, like a person inside a building. You will only be able to see the bones of the building, not who or whatever is on the other side of the walls."

Dion's eyes sparkled. "I can also freeze things. I almost can freeze Lanelle, when she's not being extra." He glared at his sister, who made a face.

"Those are all you've discovered?" Janelle asked, cutting through the sibling rivalry.

"Naw, I have super hearing too."

"What about you, Lanelle?" Janelle asked.

"Well, I have thermal vision, I can make fire and wind. Like gusts of wind. And, I can make my thoughts appear in your head."

Janelle looked at her in shock. "You're thoughts can mind jump?"

"If that's what it's called. I haven't been able to control who hears it yet. The first time, Booker and his dad was there and I did it on accident and only Booker heard."

"Whose Booker's dad?" Janelle asked as she held both hands out in front of her, doing squats.

"Mr. Benjamin," she rushed on. "And the second time I only wanted Dion to hear me but Quashawn did to too. He didn't know what was going on though." Lanelle threw out the last bit when her mother's eyes widened.

"Derek Benjamin is Booker's father?"

"Booker was in foster care since he was little. Mr. Benjamin wasn't in his life until right before he came to Douglas," Dion explained. "He is a few years older than us, he had a tough time in foster care."

"A few years?" Janelle accused.

Lanelle rolled her eyes. "Two. Two years Mother. He is only 16. We will be 15 in October.

Duante walked in the room, wearing grey sweatpants and a black muscle shirt. "Alright now," he said, clapping his hands together. "Let's get started."

Janelle straightened. "Derek Benjamin is Booker's father."

Duante's brow furrowed. Janelle said, "Dion's roommate."

Lanelle shot up. "What's that look? Tell us what's going on."

"On the floor," Janelle ordered. The family got on the floor and put on foot against the opposite thigh and reached for their foot.

"Your mother made us a team not to be messed with while we were at Douglas and later when we joined the company. She gave us an edge over all our counterparts. They noticed and were mad. Monica Michaelson, Jason Jetson, and Derek Benjamin were the three who just wouldn't let it go. Since we were seniors in high school they were always trying to expose us."

"So they were just hating that you two were good. What does that matter to us?"

Janelle shrugged. "We don't know. I am being honored by the company for career excellence. It's a coincidence that it's happening this year but maybe it's stirred some old feelings. Especially with you and your brother attending. I wonder if one of them grabbed Lanelle," she said looking at Duante.

"With that and Dion's girlfriend being sneaky," he shook his head and shrugged. "I don't know. What I do know is I do not want our children to be defenseless again. So let's go."

Anticipate my next move

"Uhh." Lanelle groaned as her back hit the mat on the hard wood in the middle of their living room.

"Up," Janelle barked. "Number one lesson in Combat is knowing how to take a hit. That's something you won't learn at Douglas."

Lanelle picked herself up off the ground and balled her fists in front of her face and she bounced slightly back and forth.

"This is not T.V. Stop bouncing," Janelle said. "You want to be standing on the balls of your feet, ready to move. Anticipate your opponent's next move and do the opposite."

"Mother, all you're doing is hitting me, and I can't even fight back."

"Defending yourself doesn't always mean attack. The best way to hide your gift from everyone is being good at defense. If you would have had a good defense, whoever wouldn't have gotten the best of you in the woods. You would have had options."

Lanelle took a deep breath and spread her feet, shoulders length apart. Putting her fists in front of her face, she focused on her mother.

Janelle's right foot was slightly in front of her left. Telling she would strike with her right. Her hands were loose at her sides.

Lanelle focused in on her arm movements. She saw when her right hand began to move and her brain slowed down the movement. She saw the flat, right hand coming at her, and stepped back with her right foot leaning out of the way. She quickly returned to her center in time to catch her mother's left hand coming at her. Her focus allowed her to see the right hand coming back up behind the left.

She's going to strike twice, she thought.

Taking a step back on her left, she ducked and shot back up and pushed on her left arm. Using her mother's momentum, she sent her staggering past her. She quickly shifted positions. Janelle swung around with a glint in her eye, shifting from the balls of her feet, down solid.

A kick is coming, Lanelle thought.

Janelle leaned to the left, brought her right foot up. and connected with Lanelle's ribs. "Grr," she grunted. The kick made her lose her focus and Janelle kicked twice more in fast succession. Lanelle flew and landed on her right shoulder hard. Hearing her mother in her ear, she ignored the pain and hopped back up.

"You lost your focus. Anticipate my next move and defend against it."

Lanelle didn't respond. A determination set in her eyes as she stood at her center position.

Janelle smirked and the kick that came at Lanelle's right rib came in slow motion. Lanelle brought her knee up to her elbow, successfully blocking the kick. Janelle squared off and brought her left leg up, kicking Lanelle in the stomach. Lanelle swiveled her hips back. A small smile crept onto Lanelle's lips.

Determined, Janelle brought her foot around, aiming for the

ribs. Lanelle picked up her leg and met her elbow, deflecting the kick again. After the next three of her kicks were blocked Janelle jabbed with an open palm and the impact threw Lanelle's head back as she stumbled.

"Anticipate my next movement," Janelle reminded her.

"I did," Lanelle groaned, throwing her hands up. "I got hit anyway."

Janelle guided Lanelle to sit on the edge of the table that was pushed to the corner of the room.

"You were doing good, but you got complacent."

Lanelle asked "I don't even know what *complacent* means Mother."

Janelle chuckled. "It means, you got comfortable with the kicks. Always remember the person you are fighting doesn't want you todefend against them. I kicked multiple times and they were blocked–"

"So it makes sense that you hit because I was expecting you to kick again," Lanelle finished.

"Exactly, and you should have anticipated that," Janelle added.

Lanelle rolled her eyes. "Yeah, okay. I get it. Anticipate your next move," she mocked.

Janelle placed her hand on Lanelle's shoulder and squeezed. "Good, now get up. Come on."

* * *

"Stop, stop, stop," Duante said. "Listen son. This isn't TV. Stop with the one two jabs. Your opponent will anticipate that. When you are attacking, you want to quickly identify the weaknesses of your opponent and then use that to your advantage."

"This is how boxers do it," Dion said, bouncing on his feet punching out in quick succession.

"This is not TV," Duante grunted.

His words had no effect on Dion who kept going like he was Muhammad Ali. Duante jaw ticked.

"Fine, you know what. Come on, we will do it our own way. Okay?"

Dion smiled wide "Aiight, cool."

They each got into their center position and Dion began bouncing back and forth with his hands protecting his face.

Out of nowhere, Duante kicked right to the ribs. Dion grunted, but before he could recover Duante had kicked him on the left. Dion stumbled slightly and got two open palmed hit to the face. That brought him to his butt with a thud.

"Dang Pop," Dion groaned.

"You're being too predictable. Every time you bounce, you give me what foot all your weight will be on and which direction you are headed. That alone leaves you open to many attacks which is how I laid you on your ass."

Dion picked himself up from the floor while flexing his jaw. "That's how everyone else does it," he countered.

"This is not TV," he repeated. "We are not playing around. Real fighting has real consequences and real injuries. Learning a good attack is only one aspect. Once you get to your mother, she will go over defense. Defense is just as important. One key element in both is anticipate the movement of your opponent and you cannot do that while jumping around. Got it?"

Dion averted his eyes and set his jaw. It ached a little. "Yeah, I got it."

"Okay," Duante said. "Get you your center protective position."

Dion stood with one foot in front of the other.

"Square off," Duante demanded.

Dion looked at his father with his feet, shoulder width apart. Hands curled up into fists in front of his face and mimicked the stance.

"Exactly," Duante encouraged. "Now you're ready to learn."

Dion narrowed his eyes and ground his teeth, not caring about the sting.

Next week then?

anelle laid on the lawn outside under a big tree. The leaves were beginning to change. Fall was her favorite season. She wore an oversized hoodie with leggings and flats. She had a scarf wrapped around her neck, more for fashion rather than warmth. She had her brother's quilt that she was laying on and played her Spotify playlist through her headphones.

The lawn was not packed today. It had been a while since she was on campus for a weekend. Her and Dion had been spending all of their weekends home training with their parents. Lanelle hated going home every weekend to be worked to the bone. She had to admit though, all the workout was making her kill it in swimming practice. With the season coming up, she should be thanking her mother.

Oblivious, Lanelle sang off key to the music only she heard when a hand came down and touched her shoulder.

Lanelle screamed and flew her arm up, releasing her wind and sent whoever was after them stumbling back. She only pushed enough to gain time to run away but she froze when she heard a scream. Lanelle's fear turned to horror as she saw Ms. Michaelson flat on her butt.

Monica giggled. "I didn't mean to startle you," she said as

she picked herself up and started wiping the leaves off.

"I am so sorry Ms. Michaelson. I didn't hear anyone come up."

Monica approached her with the warmest expression that instantly made Lanelle release a breath she didn't know she was holding.

"Oh no. I saw you had headphones in. It's no big deal. You do have quite a but of strength now don't you?"

Lanelle' forced her face not to move while she scrambled for an explanation. "I didn't do it on purpose. I swear, I just reacted."

"I'll say."

Monica looked at Lanelle for a moment. Too long. It made the warm and fuzzy feeling Lanelle felt completely disappear.

"Uhh, soo. Umm, is there something –"

Monica giggled. "Oh yes. Why am I here right?" She clasped her hands together.

Lanelle smiled awkwardly and shrugged.

"Well, I just wanted to see if you wanted to join my club for rising Freshmen. I'm the staff member overseeing it. It's only for girls and I help you jump right in and get a start on your specialties and other electives. To prepare you for your next three years."

Something in Lanelle's gut told her not to trust Ms. Michaelson.

"Well, thanks for the offer. I have a lot going on now with classes and the swim season about to start."

Monica's smile faltered for a second. So quickly that Lanelle wasn't sure she saw any change in the first place.

"Well don't answer now. You have time to think about it. I'll check in with you next week. How does that sound?"

"Okay, but I really don't think I am taking on anything new."

Apart from swimming and classes, all her and Dion's spare time was going towards training and practicing , fighting, and magic.

Monica winked. "Next week then."

While she was walking off, Lanelle tried to get comfortable again on her quilt but couldn't. She wanted to listen to her music in peace and Ms. Michaelson had ruined it.

She gathered up her things and headed back to her room.

* * *

Monica had her phone to her ear before she made it to the pavement. "Jason, I've figured it out. It's steroids."

Steroids, really?

"Monica, that doesn't make any sense." Jason said, sitting on the edge of his desk in his classroom.

"I'm telling you Jason. She flung me halfway across the lawn. What other explanation do you have for that super strength?"

Derek walked in and Monica rushed over to him. "Derek, it's steroids. They were on it when they went here and now they've got their kids on it."

One eyebrow went up and Derek looked at Jason who was rubbing his temple. Looking back at Monica he said. "Okay, explain to me your thinking?"

"She flew me halfway across the lawn. How else would she be able to do that?"

Derek's face turned serious. "Wait, she hurt you?" He said, looking her over.

"No," Jason said in frustration. "She's exaggerating. She scared the girl and got knocked over when she abruptly stood up. You know what. This is too much. I did not sign up for this. Sneaking around, following these damn kids. I would love to see Ms. Janelle get that award taken from her and let the whole company know that she cheated. Messing with these kids is not it."

Monica's eyes narrowed. "You're backing out now? We still have Imani and Booker. We know the girl is on steroids-"

"We do not know that!" Jason yelled, slamming his fists on the desk.

Monica jumped and then quickly regained composure. "You do not scare me Jason."

Jason stood and stalked over to her. Monica felt like fleeing but was determined to stand her ground.

"You sure look like you're going to piss your pants."

"Alright, enough of this," Derek said. "Come on J." Sticking his arm out in between the two.

Jason looked at Derek without moving away from Monica. "Close my door when you two are done. Don't call me again."

Monica jumped when the door slammed and took a deep breath.

"Sorry about that," Derek began.

Monica smiled slightly and tilted her head. Looking up at Derek through her lashes she cooed, "I know you believe me. Right Derek?"

"I don't know Monica."

She walked over to him and began playing with the buttons on his shirt, unbuttoning them slowly. "Don't give up on me now. Please, I don't have anyone." Drawing that last word out she slipped her hand on his chest.

"You're playing this game all by yourself," Derek said, looking down at her.

"What game?" she asked, needing playing innocently. "Can't you just help me?" she pouted, pulling her hand out and crossing her arms over her chest.

"Help you how?"

"Drug test her, then we will know."

Derek walked over and sat on the edge of Jason's desk, putting some needed space between them. "How will we get away with drug testing her?"

"Well I tried to get her to join my club, she said no because she's on the swim team. Maybe start there?" she shrugged.

Derek sighed and Monica began walking towards him. "If this doesn't work, I'm done with all this. Okay?"

"Fine," she said. *I'll just stop her on my own*, she thought.

Blush

Lanelle placed her things on the floor by her door and waved her hand. The door shut as she walked to her bed.

Taking off her scarf, hoodie. and shoes she slid a t-shirt on and grabbed her laptop before sliding on to her bed.

With the music playing through the computer speakers, Lanelle searched her favorite shopping sites. Putting things in the cart to send to her Mother to buy later when there was a knock at her door.

Focusing on the door. Lanelle saw five heat signatures and smiled. "It's open," she yelled.

Her crew walked in. "Game night," Tariana said. "It's about time you guys are here for the weekend."

"Oh, so you ready to lose?" Dion said.

Tariana rolled her eyes. "We are playing heads up boys vs. girls."

Tariana and Imani jumped on the bed. Booker went over and sat on her desk next to Quashawn. who was on the chair. He looked at Lanelle and winked.

"Well we go first," Dion said, needing snatching Tariana's phone away from her.

Tariana jumped at him. "Whatever."

After they played a few rounds, Lanelle kept looking at Booker and decided to show him what she'd learned.

Why didn't you come over earlier? She thought jumped to him. His eyes went wild and she had to stop herself from laughing. *Just think it, don't say anything out loud.*

After taking a moment to get himself together he thought, "*So this is what you've been doing all these weekends.*"

Lanelle smiled and Quashawn pushed Booker. "Yo, what are you doing? You helping or naw?

"Yeah man. Come on. Which one we on?"

"If you weren't making eyes at your girlfriend -"

Lanelle groaned. "Quashawn, chill. You always take it too far."

"Mind your business Quashawn. Whatever they do is their business," Tariana giggled.

Lanelle shoved her shoulder. "Nobody is having sex over here," she protested.

"Blah, Blah, Blah," Dion yelled over everyone.

Lanelle grabbed a pillow and threw it at him. "Grow up Dion. What you and Imani over there doing?"

Imani's cheeks turned red. Dion said, "Minding our business," while moving his neck side to side, mimicking Lanelle.

"Not by the look of those cheeks," Booker pointed out, causing everyone to look at Imani who buried her face in her hands.

"Okay D," Quashawn said.

"Naw, chill," Dion retorted. "It's not even like that."

"Can we get back to the game please?" Imani said. lifting her head up slowly.

"Yeah, the blush is gone. We can keep playing," Booker said, needing Imani to blush again. The room erupted in laughter.

* * *

Lanelle said goodbye as everyone went back to their own rooms, except Booker. "Sorry it took so long for me to get over here," he began. "I was finishing up homework so I wouldn't have any to do this weekend."

Lanelle waved her hand behind her back and the door shut. She went to go lock the door. "Haven't figured out how to do that yet," she giggled.

"So you just all types of fly now huh?"

Lanelle sat on the bed and laid against Booker's arm, holding his other hand. "Dion and I have been practicing. My parents were concerned about, uh, what happened in the woods. I don't think I told you someone grabbed me."

Booker's body tensed and he moved away to look at her "No, you didn't tell me."

Lanelle scrunched her face up. "Sorry, so when we did Adventure, Adventure someone grabbed me by the gate. They kept calling me Legacy and wanted me to do something."

Booker leaned back against the wall, putting a pillow behind his head. "Something like what?"

"I don't know, it was weird. Like they knew I could get out of the hold and wanted me to prove it." She shook her head. "Anyway, our parents said it was their fault I was unprepared and we've been training literally every second on weekends."

Booker chuckled slightly and then fell quiet. *They, whoever, called her Legacy. It couldn't be my father. Could it?*

Caught up in his thoughts, Booker didn't hear what Lanelle said. She shifted to look at him. "Booker," she called.

With a slight shake, he looked down at her. "What are you thinking?" she asked.

"About how red Imani's cheeks got," he said.

Lanelle chuckled and relaxed in his arms.

"Yeah, they doing something," she said. "Minding they business right?" she laughed.

"I would like it if we did some minding business of our own."

Lanelle tensed slightly and Booker caressed her arm. "It ain't got to be all of that. You're in control."

"I'm not no expert or nothing like you." she said.

Booker put a hand over his chest. "Was that a shot? I think that was a shot."

Lanelle laughed. "No, I didn't mean it like that. Just that," she trailed off.

Booker put his hands under her chin and lifted her head until she was looking at him. "I'm not an expert at all. And nothing I did was by choice."

"Sorry, I didn't mean to go there."

"Don't be sorry. I rather you have my story in your head. Not a made up story. You can always ask, okay?"

"Okay," she said quietly.

"Okay," he said again, focused on her.

Lanelle took a deep breath and said "Okay, again."

Booker brought his face to hers and kissed her.

Minding our business

Imani turned and went to walk to her room. Dion caught her arm. "Where you going? Booker will be here tonight. You not coming down?"

Imani's stomach fluttered "You want me to come down?" she asked, apprehensively.

"Yeah he do, y'all got some business to mind," Quashawn laughed. Tariana punched him in the arm. "We're going now. Bye y'all."

"What you mean we. You're about to go to Jacey's room, minding your business."

Tariana punched him again. "Go find you some business to mind."

Dion and Imani laughed and she looked back up at him. "It's okay. I can go back to my room."

Dion's face turned serious. "Naw, I want you to come to mine." Grabbing her hand, they headed to his room.

When they got there, he went over to his dresser and pulled out a t-shirt, throwing it at her. She caught it and smiled. "Just like old times."

He smiled and turned to look at her. His smile faded when he noticed she didn't leave the door.

"Come here," Dion sat on his bed and motioned for her to sit next to him. "I'm sorry it's taken me a long time to get over the whole bug thing. Truthfully, I had to learn to trust you again."

Imani's eyes began to water. "I'm sorry. I agreed to that before I knew y'all. He promised me I would pass his class and it would only be one thing. Then after the bug, he kept asking over and over again. I didn't want to do it. But I didn't know how to stop or how to tell you. If I knew I swear I would of."

"I know you're sorry. In the beginning, I thought you were just sorry you got caught."

Imani shook her head. "But Lanelle helped me forgive you. I been forgave you. It just took me a while to trust you again."

Imani nodded her head.

"Now quit acting like that and put that on." She smiled and pulled her shirt over her head. Dion turned and was checking his phone when Imani said, "Don't we have some business to mind?"

He dropped his phone and turned towards her. Looking at her his eyes lit up. "I mean," he said with a smile. "I'm sure I can think of a few things."

Buzz, stop flirting

The next morning, Lanelle groaned when her phone buzzed. Reaching her hand out, she flopped around on the side table trying to find her phone. Her hand hit the edge of the phone and it hit the floor with a thud.

"Dang it," she grumbled.

"Make it stop," Booker mumbled with his head under the cover.

Lanelle flung the covers off and sat up straight in the bed. Rubbing her eyes, she looked around the floor and spotted her phone. Still too lazy to walk, she reached her foot out and slid the phone closer to her with her toe. Bending over, she picked up her phone and pressed the home button, shutting the sound off.

"Oh thank God," Booker mumbled.

Lanelle was quiet for a few moments. Reading the message that had woken her up at, 7:30 in the morning!

"I have to go in for a drug test," she said astonished.

"What?" Booker asked. All the sleep out of his voice. He rolled over on the bed to look at her. Lanelle read the message. ***"Good morning Douglas High. We deeply apologize for the short notice. However, we need all students involved in any extracurricular*** *activities to come to the gym and submit to a drug test. If you do any activity outside of going to class. Clubs, groups, or sports. We need you to come to the gym immediately for a drug test."*

"Why are they making all y'all take a drug test?" Booker asked.

Lanelle turned her head to look at him. "You aren't going?"

Booker sat up in bed. Rubbing his hands through his head he said, "I don't do anything besides classes."

Lanelle looked back down at her phone.

Lanelle: You going to get drug tested?

Dion: I do the combat training after classes. Does that count as extracurricular?

Lanelle: You still do that even with doing it at home every weekend?

Dion: Just come down.

Lanelle immediately went to her dresser. She pulled some sweats over her pajama shorts. From her hamper, she pulled the hoodie she wore yesterday over her tank top. Her hand was on the doorknob when she remembered Booker was in the room. She turned around and stammered, "You uh, I mean, umm."

Booker chuckled "I'll be here when you get back."

Lanelle smiled and let out a breath before spinning and heading out the door.

Lanelle went down the stairs in a fog, busy thinking about Booker. She was so caught up in her thoughts she smacked right into someone and the impact knocked her on her butt.

"Dang girl."

"I am so sorry –" she started as she picked herself off the ground and stopped immediately when she noticed it was Dion.

Dion's eyebrows rose. "Well, I am waiting. I believe you were going to apologize to me for running into me."

Lanelle opened her mouth and then shut it again. Narrowing her eyes she said, "I'm sorry," through clenched teeth.

Dion smiled and they began walking. "What were you smiling about anyways?"

Lanelle's cheeks heated. This was one of those times she was thankful for her black skin. "Mind your business," she spat back.

Dion laughed. "Oh, so it's a mind my business type of situation?"

Lanelle sucked her teeth. "You just, ugg!" she said, not being able to think of a witty comeback.

They walked in silence for a bit. Lanelle was thankful. It gave her time to cool off. There was no way she was telling Dion anything. She didn't even want him suspecting anything. She needed to tell Booker that too. They were roommates after all.

A tall, dark skinned guy with locs walked up to us. His locs were longer than Dion's and thicker.

"What's up D," he said.

"What's up." They dapped each other up. "Do they do this often," Dion asked.

"Naw son, this is my first time." The guy responded.

Lanelle cleared her throat. "So, we just going to act like I'm not standing here?"

The guy looked over and smiled when he recognized her. "Oh what's up Shorty," he extended his hand. "Haven't seen you in a while."

Lanelle just looked at his hand. "Uh no," she said before looking up at him. "Let's try that again. I'm not your shorty and I'm sure your mother taught you manners."

Jalen smiled and stepped in front of her, stopping her from

walking. He looked at her and extended his hand again. She looked down and his hand and back up at him.

Damn those chocolate eyes, she thought. *Why does he look so familiar?*

"I'm Jalen. I know Dion from Combat and I used to do a little swimming." When he smiled, Lanelle had to stop herself from letting the *Damn* she said in her head, come out her lips.

Her eyes lit up with recognition. "That's right, you're the one who recruited me for the swim team and then disappeared."

Jalen chuckled, "I just had too much on my plate. Had to drop something."

Jalen was tall and his locs were neat, like Dion's. She couldn't stand when boys' locs were all nappy and overgrown. Like, get a retwist bruh!

Jalen's face wasn't traditionally cute. But those chocolate eyes pulled you in. She took his hand and smiled, "Hey, I'm Lanelle. Dion's sister. We're twins if you couldn't tell."

They Started walking again, but Jalen walked on the right of Lanelle and Dion stayed on the left.

"So you said you've never done a drug test here, right? What level are you?" Lanelle asked.

"I'm third level. I help Mr. Benjamin with the combat classes. But since I am still a student, it's counted as an extracurricular. Which is why I am here."

"Hmm," Lanelle said thoughtfully.

She caught Jalen staring at her when she looked up to ask another question.

"What," she giggled.

"I would say you look good. But with the two of you being twins and all, I'm not trying to complement no dude," he replied seriously.

Lanelle laughed hysterically. "Well, thanks. I think," he responded.

"Yea man, thanks," Dion said with a grin.

"Man shut up," Jalen said.

The short walk over to the gym was nice. Jalen's specialty was Combat and Protective Services. He was really good at math and wanted to be an Engineer. Dion never thought about being an Engineer and was interested when Jalen gave the overview. Lanelle had to chastise herself a few times. *You have a boyfriend* was the mantra she said in her head over and over.

Once they entered the gym it was chaos. Students everywhere are being led here and there. Lines that wrapped around each other.

At the door, there was a staff member with a clipboard. "If your last name is between A and H, you are in this line. If your last name is between I and P, use the middle lane. If your last name is between Q and Z, use the far lane."

Dion and Lanelle went to the far lane after saying goodbye to Jalen and he went to the middle lane. While in line, Dion kept looking at her.

"What?" she said.

"You know you have a boyfriend, right?"

The question caught Lanelle off guard. "What? No shit Sherlock."

"Because you were getting really friendly with him."

"Yes friendly." she scowled.

"Naw, friendly like flirting."

Lanelle rolled her eyes. "Dion, please. I am not flirting every time I talk to someone else. Chill out."

"I'm just looking out for my man Booker." Dion said, looking around the room.

"First of all, your priorities are busted. I'm your sister. Secondly, I'm a big girl with morals and values okay?"

Lanelle turned her head and crossed her arms over her chest. She didn't know whether she was mad at Dion for saying she was flirting, or mad at herself for flirting in the first place.

Drug test

I t took them almost an hour to get to the front of the line.

"This is really stupid," Lanelle said.

Monica was sitting down behind the table and overheard her. "We just have to make sure everyone is safe," she said with a smile.

"Well not everyone is here, and you woke me up at 730 am on a weekend to come stand in a line for an hour. This is so disorganized," Lanelle huffed.

Monica was about to respond when Lanelle interrupted, "Don't we have to sign something so we can go on about our business?"

Monica clenched her teeth through her smile and handed them each a pen. After signing she handed them cups. "Directions are on the cup," she said.

As they walked away, Dion heard her say, "Got you know little winch."

He jerked his head around and looked at her. Her eyes bugged wide for a moment and her smile fell back in place. "Have a good rest of your day," she said.

"She just called you a winch," Dion whispered.

Lanelle turned around and glared at her before walking into the locker room.

The staff remembers shuffled her along and collected the cup when she was done. When she walked back out of the locker room, they sent her through the back way. She didn't see Dion, so she started walking back to her building. As she came around the gym to get back to the walkway, she overheard some people whispering. She stopped and backed up the building.

Focusing her eyes, she saw two people. It was a male and a female. She cursed herself wishing she had Dion's hearing. She would have to stick her head out to actually hear what's going on.

Someone tickled her and she had to cover her mouth to stop from shrieking. She whipped around and saw Dion.

"Come here," she whispered. "It's a man and woman around the corner. Tell me what they are saying."

Dion went to go around the corner and Lanelle pulled him back.

"You don't listen," she hissed. "Just listen," she demanded. He stood still and focused.

"The man is saying, 'we have to wait until we get the results. Then we will know. No one wants to wait, just tell them to throw the other ones away and only test the Sparks.' 'Now you know we can't do that. This costs a lot of money last minute. We have to do it right. We will wait a few days and then we will have your answers.'"

Lanelle gripped Dion's arm. "They are coming, come on."

The two ran back to the door and turned around, walking the same path again. Monica and Derek reached the edge of the building before Dion and Lanelle did.

They stopped and smiled. "Good morning," they said in unison.

Lanelle gave a half smile as they walked by.

Dion and Lanelle made it to the path. "You're going back to your room?" Dion asked.

"Umm, might as well go get something to eat first. I will bring some back for Booker."

"Yeah, good Idea," Dion replied.

Lanelle raised one eyebrow. "You don't have to worry about Booker. I got him," she grinned.

Dion glanced down at her and smiled. "You know what I mean."

Lanelle pulled out her phone and added some notes down to copy into her notebook later.

Practice what I preach

L anelle showed up at her door with an armful of things from the cafe. She was going to bang her foot on the door but paused when she heard Booker talking to someone.

"You need to leave. She could be back any minute." *Okay, that was Booker's voice.* she thought.

"You had a job to do. To get any and all information on the Sparks twins. I spend half of the time tracking you down and the other half getting sent on wild goose chases."

Lanelle couldn't believe her ears. *Not just Imani, Booker too.*

Lanelle dropped the food on the floor and ran to Dion's room, her vision blurry from the tears in her eyes. She banged on his door.

"Who the hell," Dion began and stopped when he saw her.

She looked up at him and smiled, but it didn't reach her eyes.

"What's wrong?"

"Time to practice what I preach huh?" she said with a shrug.

Dion opened the door and pulled her inside. She was embarrassed when she saw Imani and Jalen in his room.

"Sorry for the interruption guys,"

"I need y'all to give us a minute," Dion said.

Imani and Jalen whispered as they headed for the door. Jalen looked at Lanelle and stopped when he was in front of her. Trying to avoid eye contact, she gave a half-hearted smile. He lifted her chin with his index finger and when she was looking at him, used his thumb to wipe her tears.

When Dion closed the door, he went over and engulfed Lanelle in a hug. She wrapped her arms around her brother and squeezed as tight as she could.

"Tell me what happened," he said into her hair.

"Booker was working with Imani, spying on us," she said into his chest.

Dion went still. "How do you know?"

"I overheard him and someone else talking in my room just now. The guy was mad at Booker because he wasn't getting the information he wanted."

"That's good right? I mean, I am not going to make you forgive him but, if whoever was mad because Booker wasn't telling him anything, that's good."

"If he wasn't telling *him* anything. Why couldn't Booker just tell *me.* I wish we would have told him about Imani. Maybe that would of gave him an opening to be honest."

"He had plenty of openings to be honest Lanelle," Dion said.

"I just need to stay here for a minute, k?"

The two stood there. Lanelle burrowed into Dion's chest for a long moment.

"Is the moment over yet?" Dion asked.

Lanelle chuckled and pushed him. "Now it is," she responded.

Lanelle plopped on the bed when there was a bang at the door.

"Dion, it's me," Imani yelled from the other side.

Dion went to open the door. "The ambulance in here. Mr. Benjamin is on his way to the hospital," she rushed out.

"Why what happened?" Lanelle asked.

"No one knows, I was waiting in the lobby for you when I saw the EMTs go upstairs. I followed them and he was on the floor in the hallway."

Dion looked back at Lanelle and she threw a thought at him. *I dropped food outside of my room. It sounds like he was the one talking to Booker and slipped when he left.*

Dion nodded slowly.

"Here they come now," Imani said. They all rushed in the hall.

The stretcher came, followed by Monica and Booker. Booker looked down the hall before walking after the stretcher. When their eyes met, Lanelle turned her head and went back into Dion's room.

Imani and Dion entered the room a few seconds later and Dion closed the door.

"I didn't mean to interrupt," Imani said, standing next to the door.

"No, it's fine. I'm okay," Lanelle insisted. "I am going to head back upstairs now," she said standing up.

"Naw, you can stay," Dion insisted.

"It's okay. I rather fall out. That drug test woke me up."

Lanelle headed for the door.

Imani fidgeted once Lanelle was gone.

"What's up?" Dion asked.

"Did she leave because of me?" Imani asked, looking up at him.

"Naw, she would have stayed if she wanted to," he chuckled. Grabbing his laptop, he went and got on the bed. "Come up here," he said.

Imani crawled up to the head of the bed. "You need a TV in here. Can't you make that happen *Legacy*?" she teased.

Dion chuckled. "Oh so I'm Legacy now. Well, when you get some TV money let me know and I'll take care of it."

Imani snorted. "Yeah okay, as soon as my mother puts the needle down long enough to give me the money, I got you."

Dion's face softened. "Damn, that's tough."

"No it's fine, I'm used to it," she rushed out. "So, what's it going to be for today?"

Dion began to scroll through his streaming services to find a movie.

* * *

Lanelle walked down the hallway towards her room. She deflated when she saw the mess of food outside the door.

"I didn't mean for anyone to get hurt, I just wasn't thinking straight," she mumbled. Turning around she went to the janitor's closet and got the broom and the mop. After she cleaned up the mess and put the supplies back, she headed to her room.

Waving the door shut, her body felt so heavy and she collapsed on the bed. She was overwhelmed with the sense of betrayal she felt and the sense of guilt for feeling betrayed after saying all that stuff to Dion about Imani. Could she take her own advice?

Lanelle didn't know how long she laid there, spreadeagle on the bed. She just couldn't get her thoughts straight, couldn't separate her thoughts from her feelings. Because her feelings were telling her to burn all his things.

She groaned aloud.

There was a knock at the door.

She lifted her head, with much effort and focused on the door.

One male.

Probably Booker.

She didn't want to answer it.

Her head flopped back down.

A few moments later, her phone buzzed. Her limbs felt too heavy to go searching for it, so she didn't. Her phone buzzed again and she cursed before moving her body to get it out of her pocket.

Booker: Let me in please

Booker: We have to talk

She assumed he'd left. Focusing back on the door, she saw his heat signature low to the ground, sitting maybe but further away from the door. Lanelle sighed and knew she would have to let him in. The guilt over being upset and the lectures she gave Dion were eating at her.

She picked up her phone and typed back ***It's open***. She didn't have the strength to talk. It seemed her body and voice just wanted to collapse.

The door opened and Booker came in, looking depressed.

Depressed because he got caught or depressed because he knows he hurt me, she thought.

He closed the door behind him and leaned back on it.

"Just let me explain," he said after a moment.

Lanelle didn't respond. She was flat on her back on the bed looking up at the ceiling, waiting for him.

When he caught on, he said, "I didn't even know who he was until last year, a few months before school ended. I came home from school and the group home said I had a visitor. This man walked up and told me his name was Derek and he had been partitioning the court to let me come down to North Carolina to go to school here for high school and the court finally approved.”

Booker stopped, waiting for her to say something, or maybe he was waiting for her to acknowledge him, but she didn't. She stayed in one spot, arms and legs spread out and looking at the ceiling.

She didn't notice that his nails were biting into his skin so hard he drew blood.

“Anyway, I found out that he was my Father, and he was now my guardian. He claimed he didn't know I existed and had no clue where my mother was. So, I ended up here, in North Carolina stuck in between hating this man who abandoned me my whole life and desperately needing his approval.”

Lanelle's heart broke, but didn't move or respond though. Growing up, she knew she was blessed to have both parents around. Even the white kids in her school, most of them only had one parent. She used to get embarrassed when her mother would show up to all the events and meetings. Later, she found out that's why she was getting into so many fights. The other kids were jealous that she had a mom and tried to bully her. However, Lanelle wasn't a punk and she would not let anyone bully her. Booker's voice pulled her from her thoughts.

“A few days before orientation started. He told me my roommate would be someone named Dion Sparks, he and his twin sister were new students. That he needed me to become friends with Dion and tell him anything I found out. He said he had the sister taken care of, someone else would be friends with her. He just needed me close to Dion. I felt weird about it at first, but I agreed. Until I met y'all that first day and I knew I couldn't do it.”

That was a lot to digest, Lanelle thought. *So, Imani was supposed to get close to me, not Dion. That made sense. Why would they have someone in the room with Dion and listening to all the conversations too?*

"I go to therapy once a week. I have for as long as I could remember. She helped me understand the need for approval, which is why I agreed in the first place. And she also helped me understand that I had no real connection with Derek. The acceptance I felt from y'all made me feel more connected to you than to him. Which is why I haven't told him anything."

Then something clicked. "He knows about my gift," Lanelle mumbled laying on the bed, when all the pieces began clicking in her head. "Him, Michaelson, Jetson. They all know about our magic. They just need proof in order to expose us."

Booker stood up straight. "I didn't tell him anything about anything. Especially about the magic I swear. Lanelle, please believe me."

She shook her head. "There is one side that believes I have to. We found out Imani had bugged your room. She's the other one your father was talking about, but she got close to the wrong twin. But, I told Dion all this stuff about forgiveness, intentions, and heart. How can I, after feeding all that stuff to Dion, sit here and not forgive you? Then on the other hand. You had so many opportunities to tell me and you didn't. How am I supposed to feel about that?"

Booker was shocked when he heard about Imani. Derek never told him who the other student was, just that there was another one. He looked at Lanelle and his heart broke. She looked exhausted laying there.

Lanelle's head swamped with all the information she was taking in. "I need Dion. Can you call him up here please?" she asked softly.

Booker took the opportunity to leave and get Dion himself.

Lanelle was confused when she heard the door shut and lifted her head.

"He left," she said aloud. She was grateful for it though. It gave her time to think.

It all makes sense

Lanelle took a few minutes to update her notebook and then collapsed back on the bed.

Dion and Booker came into Lanelle's room. She had not moved on her bed.

"Come on Lanelle, get up. You've been like this the whole time?"

Lanelle frowned. "How would you know how I've been the whole time?"

"Booker told me, now get up," Dion said again.

Lanelle groaned and slid up the bed until she was leaning against the wall. She hugged her knees.

"So am I playing mediator or what?" Dion asked.

"No, I just need you to listen. Booker and Imani were supposed to get close to us. They were sent by Benjamin and Jetson. The only issue was they got close to the wrong twin."

Dion nodded his head. "Okay, so."

"Dion, it doesn't make any sense for Benjamin to ask Booker to spy on you and have Imani put a bug in your room too."

"Right, so Imani was supposed to become your best friend or something?"

Lanelle sat up a little straighter. "Right, remember the first night? She is the one who introduced herself to me. She came here. So Benjamin, Jetson, and Michaelson have a serious issue with us."

"Hold on," Dion said, waving his hands. "How did we get Michaelson? I know Jetson because he is the one I caught Imani arguing with."

"Remember the drug test? Benjamin and Michaelson were whispering behind the building. She has to be in on it. She just gives me a weird feeling."

Dion took a moment to process and turned to Booker. "What did your father tell you about why you were supposed to spy on me?"

Booker groaned at your *father* title. "He didn't give me any details. All he told me was I was roommates with you, he needed me to become tight, and tell him anything you told me."

"Imani should be here," Dion said, pulling his phone out.

"No!" Lanelle said jumping forward.

"Why not?" Dion asked, confused.

"Think about it, Dion. Why would three teachers be so focused on us? What makes us different from everyone else?"

Dion thought for a moment and then nodded his head when he caught up. "Legacy," he said.

"Right -"

"What does our parents have to do with Imani?" Dion asked, still confused.

Lanelle growled in frustration. "Have you told Imani about what we can do?"

"Of course not," Dion said immediately.

"Booker already knows and why else would these three teachers be so focused on us? They know Dion. Maybe all the way back from our parents, but they know. They just need proof. That's why they got everyone to spy on us."

Dion turned and looked at Booker, narrowing his eyes. "You told your father about-"

"Naw man," Booker held his hands in a surrender motion.

"Call him Benjamin, Dion. Not *your father,*" She mocked.

Booker was relieved she saw his discomfort every time Dion said that. That gave him hope that she would forgive him.

Dion looked at Lanelle and then back at Booker. "What did you tell him?"

"Nothing, honestly. Every time he showed up, we fought because I told him I wasn't playing his game anymore."

"What did you guys talk about when the bug was in your room?"

The room went silent.

"I never asked her when she did it," Dion said.

"I didn't even know it was there until just now," Booker replied.

"Did you guys ever talk about magic or anything?"

Dion sat cross legged on the bed next to Lanelle.

"It doesn't make sense. Why would they have it out for us before the school year even started. They don't even know us?"

The three were quiet for a moment when Dion's face lit up. "The award," he said.

Lanelle furrowed her brows. "What does that have to do with anything?"

"Do you think Ma' would get the award still if it was discovered we were cheating in some way?"

Booker screwed his face up. "I'm confused. Why does it matter to them whether she gets an award or not?"

"Who is next in line for the award?' Lanelle asked. Both boys shrugged their shoulders.

"We need to find that out. I bet it's either Benjamin, Michaelson, or Jetson."

"And how do we do that?" Dion asked.

Lanelle shook her head slightly, widening her eyes, "Why do I have to do all the work? I don't know."

Dion groaned and pushed her.

"I'll see what I can find out," Booker said hesitantly.

Booker and Dion looked at Lanelle.

"Yeah, that's cool," she said.

Dion stood up. "Okay, I'm out," he said, holding both his deuces up.

He rushed out the room and shut the door. Dion leaving brought the tension and awkwardness back into the room and it suffocated Lanelle. She slowly slid back to a prone position on the bed.

"Uhh, I can leave and talk to you later," Booker said after a few moments.

Lanelle was quiet for a moment and sighed.

"I want you here more than I am mad at you." She shook her head. "I'm not even mad but betrayed. I'm battling losing trust. Which is making me mad because that is exactly what Dion said to me a few months ago. And I told him to look at her intentions. Who is the person he knows, not the person he sees because of being hurt."

Booker's shoulders slumped. "I'm sorry."

Lanelle let the apology move around her head. Was it enough?

"Plus, Imani is downstairs. I think you have officially been kicked out of your room."

Booker let out a breath at her attempted humor.

"Come on," she said, patting the bed next to her.

Booker slipped out of his shoes and shirt and climbed in next to her. She reached over and grabbed her laptop.

"You need a TV," Booker said.

"I know! But my parents are going to have to buy two and that ain't happening."

"Maybe I'll buy one for you."

Lanelle turned and looked at him. "Where you got TV money?"

"I'll just tell Derek to get it for me," he said shrugging.

Her features soften, "You don't have to do that. We'll struggle until we can get one."

Booker started laughing. "That's what this is, struggling?"

Surprise

L anelle and Dion were in her room, searching online for clothes. Their parents had given them $100 each for their birthday.

"I'm getting these Jordans'," Dion said.

"Whatever Jordans' you're looking at for under $100 are fake."

Dion sucked his teeth. "I'm using the money I had saved to, dang. Mind ya business."

"Okay, and when they start peeling, I won't say I told you so."

Dion pushed her and Lanelle began to laugh. Her three carts were filled with make-up and clothes. They all totaled $250. So she had to re-evaluate too.

There was a knock at the door. Lanelle glanced up and focused.

"That's weird," she said.

"What?"

"The heat signatures look all weird," she said as she got up and went to the door.

When she opened it there was a unison "Happy Birthday!" which made her jump. Their parents, and mother's parents were there with two big boxes.

"Move aside and let us in," Darius, Janelle's father said.

Lanelle smiled and let everyone in the room.

"Couldn't see us because of these boxes huh?" Shanelle, Janelle's mom asked in her thick Jamaican accent. "Found that trick out a long time ago. Holding something big like these boxes messes up your little vision," she continued.

"Come here boy, sitting there acting like you're too good to give Grandpa D a hug." Darius said, gesturing to Dion. Dion smiled and stood to hug his grandparents.

"So, what's in the boxes?" Dion asked.

"Well," Janelle began, "you are going to help your father and grandfather take yours to your room. You can open it there."

At the mention of their father, both Lanelle and Dion whipped their heads around.

Duante began to laugh. "Oh y'all forgot about me huh?"

Both went to go hug him. "Naw, I don't want no pity hug," He said with mock offense.

"Come grab this box boy," Darius said.

Dion went over and grabbed the big box. Him, Duante, and Darius left the room.

"So I can open mine now, right?" Lanelle asked barely containing herself.

Janelle chuckled. "Go ahead," she said.

Lanelle tore into the box and shrieked when she saw the TV on the box.

"We got TV's. Thanks Mother!" she said and ran to give her mother a hug. "Booker will set it up later," Lanelle said more to herself than her mother and grandmother.

"Who is this Booker person? "Shanelle said.

Lanelle groaned. "Grandma Nelle."

"It's okay Mom, you will meet him at the Halloween party

tonight."

Lanelle's eyes got wide as she turned towards her mother. "How, where," she stuttered.

Janelle laughed. "It's in the gym tonight. We got it approved with the Dean."

"I need nails, and an outfit, two outfits. I have to do a costume change and my hair." Her hands flew to her two puffs. "Mother, what about my hair? What am I going to do about these puffs?"

Shanelle and Janelle were giggling. "Slow down girl. We got you covered," Shanelle said.

Lanelle smiled. "Y'all got me covered," she repeated mimicking her grandmother's accent.

* * *

Dion jumped up in the air. "Yes!" he yelled, quickly unwrapping the rest of the paper. "We can put this up now right?" he asked, looking back and forth from Darius to Duante.

Duante chuckled. "We have things to do first."

Dion ripped open the television box. "What could be more important than getting this TV up?

"There seems to be a party tonight. Your mother told us to get you ready for. Your dad has a checklist," Darius said.

Dion froze and looked up. "You're serious."

Duante smiled. "We got permission to use the gym. Your friends helped up set it up."

Dion jumped up. "Come on, I need a costume. Wait, two. You know Lanelle is going to get two. Are we going home? I need a retwist and –"

Duante and Darius laughed as they stood. "Slow down boy," Darius said. "Your mother gave us a list we got it covered."

Dion grabbed his phone and video called Lanelle.

"Hey, are we matching?" He said, once she picked up.

"Let's do Disney Villains. Jasmine and Jafar and Tiana and Facilier."

Dion furrowed his brow. "Who is Facilier and Tiana?"

Lanelle rolled her eyes. "From Princess And The Frog."

"Why can't we do Beauty and the Beast?"

Lanelle gave an 'are you serious' look in the camera. "No white princesses Dion. Now make sure you get the right costumes. You need me to say it again. Or should I text it to you."

Dion let out an exaggerated sigh "Jafar and Facilier, got it."

Lanelle smiled wide. "I'm going to text you anyway. Bye."

Halloween

The gym became a haunted house. There were spiderwebs on the doors with spiders in them. Fog machines filled the room with smoke. The lights were off and there were glowing ghosts around the gym, making everything glimmer. There were zombies, vampires, and skeletons, balloons, and streamers everywhere. There was a DJ and an ice cream bar.

"This is what I'm talking about," Dion said.

Janelle signaled the DJ and Stevie Wonders *Happy Birthday* started playing and the whole gym joined in.

"There are so many people here," Lanelle said. "How did this happen without us knowing?"

Dion leaned over and whispered to her. "Well, Imani and Booker are good at keeping secrets."

Lanelle glared at him. "Not funny."

All of a sudden, the song changed to *Birthday Chick* by Trap Beckham. Dion and Lanelle looked at each other and walked into the crowd, dancing.

The beat dropped and the whole gym was dancing.

After the song finished everyone was coming up to the twins saying happy birthday. They smiled, thanked everyone, and finally spotted their crew.

"How many of you knew?" Lanelle asked, finger pointed at them.

Tariana, Booker, Imani and Quashawn made zipping motions on their lips.

"Okay, Okay I see how it is," she said laughing.

Imani was dressed as Thunder and Tariana was dressed as Lightning from Black Lightning. She came up and grabbed Tariana and Lanelle's hand. "Let's go take pictures." The girls walked off.

Booker and Quashawn were dressed as Black Panther.

"Dang, we should have been superheroes," Dion said.

Booker leaned in. "Your mother said that Lanelle was going to make you do Disney. You know how Lanelle feels about black characters and I wasn't going to be an Asian guy so," he gestured to his outfit. "Superheroes it is,"

Dion laughed. "This is tight though. She loves it."

Quashawn put his arm around Dion's shoulder. "Okay I understand the sister thing, I do, but do you like it? It's your birthday too, remember."

Dion grinned. "Yea, y'all did iight," Dion said, exaggerating the last word.

The three started laughing. "I swore Imani was going to tell you," Booker said.

"They were too busy for talking when they were in that room," Quashawn grinned.

Dion sucked his teeth. "I swear y'all need to mind ya business. Don't worry ain't nothing happening over here that you two ain't doing."

"Please, I don't know about you two, but I still sleep in my own bed," Quashawn said.

"Lies," Booker and Dion said together.

Quashawn laughed as Tariana came back. "Lanelle wants pictures, come on," she said and was gone before they could respond.

* * *

Janelle and Duante went over to the dry bar and got a soda. Darius and Shanelle were still on the dance floor going.

"How do they have more stamina than us?" Duante asked.

Janelle laughed and opened her mouth to respond when she saw Monica and Derek headed her way. She quickly snapped it shut.

Monica was dressed in a wedding dress with blood dripping down it and Derek was a pirate.

Monica smiled wide. "Hey Sparks. This is a great thing you did for your kids. It's almost like everyone here is here for them and not just because it's a party with free food."

Derek grabbed her arm and squeezed.

"And your costume is cute. Who are you, the black Wonder Woman?"

Derek squeezed her arm harder and she failed at trying to yank it away.

"Duante, you must be. Hmm I don't know. Dressed tacky maybe."

Janelle smiled. "Poor thing. I know you have been struggling all these years without anyone to hate on. It must have been hard on you, Duante and I leaving and settling down, having a family. I'll give you that pass. You are looking at Nu'Bia and Prince Akeem."

"From Coming to America," Derek said with a smirk.

Duante nodded his head.

"I don't even know who they are," Monica sniffed. "You were too poor to get good costumes."

"No Monica, that just means you're uncultured." Janelle snapped.

Suddenly Lanelle and Dion popped up. Lanelle glared at Monica.

"Ms. Michaelson, have the drug tests come back yet? It's been a couple weeks and we haven't heard anything."

Monica looked at her. "Um, yes they have."

"Oh, they must have come back negative. That's why we didn't hear about them." Lanelle replied.

Monica smiled and before she could respond, Dion spoke up. "Naw, we don't want that smile. Keep that same energy you had talking to my parents. Or that same energy you had taken to Benjamin behind the gym. Or that same energy you had telling Booker and Imani to spy on us."

Janelle stepped within inches of Monica. "And when I ruin your career with my thank you speech for fucking with kids, bring that same energy."

Monica squinted her eyes and squared her shoulders.

"Now ladies, whatever this, now it is not the place or time," Shanelle shouted, her accent floating through the group of people.

"You better remember who she is stepping to like that," Dion said.

"Lanelle, Dion, go join your friends and enjoy your party."

They knew it wasn't a request, it was a demand. With one last look at Monica and Derek, they turned and headed back to the dance floor.

"You won't get to say that speech. I'll prove you cheated, and I'll prove your kids are cheating. There is no way you could have been that good. I deserve this award, not you."

Janelle smiled. "See you next month Monica." She winked and walked away.

Monica went to follow but Duante's glare stopped her in her tracks.

She was mad, but not stupid. She did remember who they were and how good they were. It was time for her to start playing dirty.

"I'm done Monica," Derek said.

Monica snapped her gaze towards him.

"I told you if the drug tests didn't work, I was done. I'm done with the wild goose chase, plus my relationship with my son is broken."

"Pssh, you don't care about that boy. You left him in foster care for 15 years," Monica spat.

Derek jerked back with the slap of her words. He slowly nodded his head. "Enjoy the party Monica."

"I don't need you. I don't need Jason. I will stop her from getting that award by my damn self."

Kids walking past started looking at Monica and she realized where she was. Straightening her shoulders, she headed back into the crowd. They would not run her out. She was Monica Michaelson dammit, she was this damn company.

The party goes on

Lanelle, Tariana, and Imani headed to the bathroom.

"This is fun. Thank you for setting this up with my parents." Lanelle went into one of the stalls.

Tariana and Imani stayed in the mirror.

"Girl, I was surprised when Imani came to me saying your mother sent her a Facebook message. It was hard keeping it a secret. It was really Booker though. He did most of the work for the past few weeks."

Lanelle wondered if it was mainly because of his guilt. She shook her head to dislodge that thought. She was working on trusting him and things were going well.

Lanelle flushed and came out of the bathroom, adjusting her outfit. "Time for a costume change," she exclaimed.

The Jasmine outfit was easy enough to get out of, but the Tiana dress would take some work.

Imani ran back in with the second costume. "I told Dion it was time to change too."

Ten minutes later, the girls went back to the gym and straight to the dance floor.

The crew was in a group dancing and having a good time when Jacey came and grabbed Tariana to dance.

Lanelle looked at her and grinned.

"May I have this dance," someone said from behind her.

She twirled around Jalen. Lanelle admired his boxer costume.

"Sure," she said and the two of them started dancing to the upbeat song.

She was having such a good time that she forgot about Booker and whether she should be dancing with someone else. The thought made her hesitate and she decided to pretend she needed a break.

"Getting old, huh?" he said.

She put her hands on her hips in mock offense.

Behind her Dion pushed Booker towards Lanelle. He came up behind her. "My turn yet?"

Lanelle turned her head and smiled. "Booker, this is Jalen. Jalen. Booker."

The two gave each other a head nod. "Alright birthday girl, I'll see you later." Jalen said and then walked off.

Lanelle smiled and turned to dance with Booker.

"Who was that?" he asked.

"He's third level. He does that Combat thing with Dion."

Booker nodded his head. The song slowed and everyone began swaying back and forth. Lanelle settled into Booker's shoulder.

"That must be why he doesn't look familiar. I don't mess with third levels a lot."

Lanelle began to get nervous. "I've only seen him a few times. Not until we had that drug test though."

Booker stayed quiet and that made her even more nervous. She looked up at him and saw the turmoil in his eyes when he looked back down at her.

"What's on your mind?" she asked.

He shook his head. "Are you enjoying your party?"

"Don't change the subject. What's on your mind?"

Booker was quiet for a moment. "Don't want someone else slipping in and taking my spot."

Bring on the guilt. Yeah, Lanelle was attracted to Jalen. That was just because he looked good, not because she was trying to replace Booker. She met him before she found out Booker had been lying.

"There is nothing for you to worry about. If anything, I would tell you."

"Really, you would?" Booker asked.

Her heart broke at his vulnerability.

"Really," she said and laid her head back on his shoulder.

Okay Lanelle, stop being a jerk.

As the night came to an end, Lanelle and Dion made their rounds, thanking everyone for coming. Some of these kids have never seen a day in their lives. Guess there was nothing else to do around Douglas.

The crew began taking down the decorations and cleaning up the gym.

Monica was one of the last adults, except for family, left in the gym. She paused in front of Janelle, "Couldn't you hire someone to do this?"

"Chile, would you go on please?" Shanelle's accent was thick.

Monica looked taken aback.

"Let my child enjoy her children's birthday. Go on now," Shanelle chastised.

Janelle glared at her, daring her to respond.

Monica sucked her teeth and walked out of the gym.

"We should talk to the kids about her," Duante said.

Janelle sighed heavily. "Yeah. She's going to come at them hard now."

"Knowing your daughter, she will try to come back. We need

to talk to them before we leave."

The gym was almost clean, and the crew and the family were the only ones left in the gym. A few of Lanelle's friends from classes helped clean up a little bit. Jalen and Jacey were still around too.

"So, you guys need to put that $100 in your savings," Duante said.

Lanelle's mouth dropped open and Dion said, "Come on pops."

Duante chuckled. "I'm serious. You've had a great day. Save the money."

"That's a request right, not a demand?" Lanelle asked.

"We would love it if you saved it," Janelle jumped in. "But it is a request."

Lanelle let out a breath. "Okay good."

The parents and grandparents begin to laugh.

"Say goodnight to your friends. You father and I have to talk to you before we head home," Janelle said.

Behave

anelle and Dion took about an hour to take off their costumes and change. Lanelle put on a t-shirt and yoga pants and Dion changed into sweatpants and a t-shirt. Dion came up to Lanelle's room and opened the door. Lanelle was startled by the door opening and waved it shut.

"Dang," Dion exclaimed.

"Can't you knock?" she said, making a face at him.

"So, you beat me with the door? Because that makes sense."

"You could have been someone coming to kill me. Like, Michaelson. You could have been Michaelson," She said with resolve.

"And your response to Michaelson is to magically beat her with the door?" He asked, raising his voice for emphasis.

"Enough now, enough. Come tell Grandma Nelle bye now," Shanelle said, as she stood from Lanelle's bed.

The twins went over and gave their grandparents hugs and said goodbye.

Once the door shut Lanelle went to sit on her bed cross legged. "So what did we do?"

"You tell us?" Duante said.

"The last time we had one of these conversations we ended up in boarding school," Dion said, going to sit next to Lanelle.

Duante went and sat on the desk while Janelle took the chair and brought it to the end of the bed.

"We need you two to leave Monica alone."

Lanelle sucked her teeth. "Mother, we don't even mess with her. She's the one who is messing with our lives."

"No pranks, no disrespect, nothing like that. She is obviously a little bitter that your mother is winning the career award. She might be petty and we need you guys to leave her alone," Duante said.

Lanelle sat back and crossed her arms over her chest.

"Lanelle," Janelle started. "You have to trust us to handle this."

"From home!" she screeched, outstretching her arms. "How are you going to in one breath teach us how to defend our ourselves and control and in the next breath tell us to leave her alone?"

"You better watch who you're speaking to," Duante said "that tone is unacceptable."

Lanelle huffed and crossed her arms again. "Fine."

"This is grown folks' business," Janelle said.

"But Ma, you're talking like we brought this on ourselves. She had people set up to spy on up before we even go here."

"I know, and you guys did a great job forgiving your friends."

Lanelle really felt like rolling her eyes, but she valued her life, so she decided against it.

Janelle continued. "We are sorry you guys are caught in the middle of this. At the time, we didn't think using my gifts on missions would have this big of an impact 15 years later."

Everyone looked at Lanelle. "I said fine," she said in a clipped tone.

"Lanelle, don't get into one of your moods," Dion scowled.

"Too late," Lanelle countered.

Dion sighed exaggeratedly.

Janelle stood up. "Okay, this is as far as we are getting tonight. So, we will head home and see you guys this weekend."

Dion got up to hug her. "Bye Ma, bye Pops."

Lanelle got up and hugged her parents silently. Dion sighed and said goodbye one final time before leaving.

"Send Booker up please," Lanelle said after him. "He has to set up my TV," she added quickly when her father gave her a look.

* * *

Booker picked up the remote and turned the tv on. Lanelle put her hands in the air in victory when it turned on.

"We should be able to use the school's Wi-Fi and log on to the apps using the username and password you use at home," Booker said, handing Lanelle the remote.

"What is there to watch on BET?" Booker asked.

"I have to catch up on 'Love and Hip Hop.' I haven't been home in a while to watch it," Lanelle said matter of factly.

Booker groaned and pulled the pillow over his head. "So. we're about to watch ratchet TV all night?" His voice was muffled by the pillow.

Lanelle stared at him through downturned eyes. "Stop acting like that."

Booker groaned and sat up in the bed. "What did your parents have to talk to y'all about?"

"Basically, that Michaelson is going to start coming for Dion and I and we need to be nice and leave her alone."

"Damn really?" he responded.

"I know right. We got the whole 'this isn't a request' thing and, urg! They get on my nerves."

Booker was quiet for a moment. "Derek came by today, after the dance."

Lanelle paused before hitting the play button. "What happened?"

Booker played with the edge of the blanket, not making eye contact. "He apologized for everything, basically. Told me he always knew he wanted me to be at Douglas and really didn't know I was in Foster Care or where my mother was. Told me he could have cared before I was 15. Apologized for putting me in the position with you and Dion. He said what he was trying to do doesn't seem as important now as it did when this all started."

"How does that make you feel? And how is he? He looked fine at the dance today."

Booker still played with the blanket. "He didn't break it or anything. He told me I overreacted by calling 911, I should have just called the nurse."

"How does it all make you feel?" Lanelle asked again.

Booker inhaled and exhaled deeply. "I don't know. I go see my therapist in two days. Maybe I will have to talk through it with her."

That felt like a slap in the face, she thought. *Why can't he talk to me?* She wondered.

A few moments of awkward silence passed, and she picked up the remote again.

"Yeah, I don't know," he said again.

Here we go

Dion and Imani were sitting on his bed, watching TV. Dion was slumped over. Imani was sure he was sleeping.

"It was great being with your family today," Imani said quietly.

Dion stirred a little but didn't seem to wake up, so she continued.

"My mom has been on drugs for as long as I can remember. My father tried but the drugs were too much for him to handle and he left. I must have been too much for him to handle too."

She was quiet for a while and Dion thought that she was done. He still laid there. Pretending to be sleep seemed to be giving her the courage she needed to express herself.

"It kind of made me sad," she finally continued. "Seeing you and your parents and grandparents. I don't even know if my grandparents are alive. I've had to take care of my mom since I was like seven."

She sounded like she was crying. Dion wanted to reach out and hold her, but didn't want her to stop talking. It was kind of selfish really. He just wanted to know her story.

"I don't even know how I came across this school. You have to be referred ya' know. There are a lot of Legacies. I mean a lot.

The other students get recommended by an aunt or someone working in the company. There aren't a lot of charity stories like me though."

Dion stirred and Imani tensed up. He decided to just lay there until she was done. Just let her speak.

"When you guys welcomed me, I felt like I finally belonged. I felt like shit for only introducing myself because Jetson asked. I didn't know what I would do when you got mad at me."

Dion's phone buzzed and she quickly wiped her face. He was stuck, didn't know what to do.

"I see you," he said when he sat up. He decided it was better just to be up front with her.

Imani started sobbing into his shoulder and they stayed there for a moment.

* * *

The building was quiet when everyone's phone began that buzzing sound that happened when the message went out for the drug test.

Douglas Alert: Good evening Douglas High. Please stand outside of your door for count.

Booker peeked at his phone through one eye. "What is count?" he asked in a hazy voice. Suddenly, there was a bang on their door.

"Guys, it's Imani. Open the door."

She knocked until Lanelle finally opened the door. "Who died?" she yawned.

"Count means you have to be outside of your door. It is against school rules to be staying in someone else's room. Booker," she said peeking her head around Lanelle. "Get downstairs now!" and she turned and hurried to her room.

Lanelle turned towards Booker. "Don't worry about a shirt, you have them in your room, just go."

Lanelle was standing outside her room when Monica and a few other teachers came walking down the hall. *Does she sleep here?* Lanelle thought. She watched Ms. Michaelson and the other staff stop by each person's room, check their paper, and glanced inside the open door.

When Michaelson began walking towards Lanelle, she turned her head and looked straight on. Her mother telling her to be nice on repeat in her head.

"Well hello Ms. Sparks. A bit underdressed are we?"

Lanelle looked down at her short shorts and tank top without a bra. "It is the middle of the night Ms. Michaelson," she said with the sweetest tone she could muster.

Monica's smile dropped. "Open your door please?"

Lanelle was surprised by the request and stared at her for a moment before complying hesitantly.

"Don't worry Ms. Sparks, we can't go in without parent permission. We just want to make sure everything is in order. We've seen all types of messes before," The teacher laughed; what she said was meant to be a joke, but Monica stiffened and froze about two steps before she entered Lanelle's room.

She spoiled your plan, didn't she? Lanelle thought and smirked. "Thanks," she told the teacher, making sure Monica saw the smile on her face. "Glad to know Douglas cares about my privacy."

The teacher smiled and checked her clipboard one more time.

"Okay Ms. Michaelson, we are ready to move on."

Monica got real close to Lanelle's face. "I hope you don't think you've won something," Monica whispered.

Lanelle looked up, with a pleasant grin. "I hope you didn't wake up the entire school just to try to illegally search my room. I wonder what the Dean, or better yet my mother will think about that?"

Monica stiffened and glared at her.

"You do not scare me child. Whatever your family is hiding, I will figure it out."

"You're a bit bitter Ms. Michaelson. My mother was a better agent than you 15 years ago and you still haven't come to terms with being second best?" Lanelle made tsk sounds with her mouth. "I hope you get over it in time for the award ceremony."

"You mean *my* award ceremony."

Without another word she turned, flipped her hair, and walked down the hall.

Once the teachers left the hall, everyone turned and went back into their rooms.

Lanelle went and jumped on her bed and pulled her notebook from off the side table. She added 'tried to search my room' under the list of things Ms. Michaelson has done to her.

I'm late

The week flew by. There hasn't been enough time to complete all the work the teachers gave out, let alone do anything else.

Ms. Michelson gave too much homework every day. Possibly on purpose, but she gave it to the whole class, not just Lanelle.

Lanelle was late from the library to her swim meet. Rushing through campus with her backpack, half open and books in her hand, she swerves through people walking, sitting down, and just going too slow.

She doesn't know if she's dropping things out her bag and can't spare the time to turn and look back.

In the library, she had to put her hair in a messy puff-tail because her curls were getting in her face. Then she kicked herself and remembered she should have put it in two French braids for the meet today. There was no way she was going to fit her hair into that swim cap without braiding it first.

Bursting through the pool doors, everyone spun to look at her. Her coach gave her a look and Lanelle looked back apologetically but kept going towards the lockers.

"Five minutes," the coach yelled after her.

The spectators would start filing in any moment now. Even though this is just practice. Coach told the team to treat it like a real meet, which means don't be late.

Lanelle crashed into the locker rooms and dumped all her stuff on the floor. She turned her backpack upside down until her bathing suit and cap fell out. Everyone wore a navy blue swimsuit because Douglas' colors were navy blue and silver.

I hope no one comes in, I hope no one comes in, Lanelle thought repeatedly in her head as she kicked her shoes off and shimmied out of her pants and panties. She quickly bent down to pick up her bathing suit and stepped into it, bringing it to her waist as she shook her hair loose and pulled on half of it and started braiding.

When she finished one braid, she yanked her shirt over her head and reached behind her to pull her bra off. Once the latch unhooked, she yanked her bathing suit the rest of the way up and let out a breath she didn't know she was holding. She grabbed her swim cap and stuffed it under her arm and began braiding the other half of her hair.

By the time she got to the locker room door she was stuffing her hair into the swim cap. She raced out and got in the pool with the rest of her team in time to hear Coach's speech.

Glancing sideways at her Coach continued. "We all know this is practice but we have made it as realistic as possible. There are judges, a crowd, and there will be a winner. I need every one of you to treat this as real as possible."

Everyone swam off to get ready for the start. Lanelle wasn't going first, so she went over and sat with the rest of the team on the side. She finally got a chance to look at the crowd and smiled when she saw her crew, and Jalen. A grin extended over her face. Then she quickly cursed herself.

Come on Lanelle, get over yourself.

She spun around and sat on the bench. Glad her skin was too

dark to blush.

When it was time for Lanelle to compete, she was confident. Even before she came into her powers, she excelled at swimming. Now it was even better. She used her hands as propellers. Every time she moved, she pushed herself forward. Going way further than she ever could if she didn't use her powers.

She stood in place and listened for the shot to signify the race has begun. As soon as the sound reached her ears, she jumped in. She did the first few strokes regular and then used her wind to propel herself forward. Gaining yards on her competition with each stroke.

She tapped the wall, went under, and turned around. Not giving in to glancing at her opponents. she just put more power into her strokes. Commanded the wind to move her forward harder and farther. When her fingers hit the wall again, she bounded upward to look around.

The crowd was clapping, giving her a standing ovation. Her gaze found Jalen first and guilt hit her in the chest so hard she couldn't take a deep breath. She searched and found Booker. He was standing next to Dion and Quashawn and they were making all this noise; whooping and clapping. Tariana and Imani were screeching and jumping up and down.

Lanelle loved swimming. She loved how she felt in the water and that she was good at something by herself. Growing up with Dion meant that everyone automatically put them together.

The twins this and the twins that. The twins took karate and dance class. The twins did track and book club. Dion wasn't a good swimmer and did not like it as a sport. So it was just hers. Not Dion and Lanelle but just Lanelle.

"Hey Sparks, don't gloat and get out of the water," Coach yelled, bringing her back to the present. As she walked back to her seat she looked back up at the crowd. More people were standing and cheering since the rest of the team had finished. It was time for the boys and then the second event, which Lanelle wasn't in, so she had little break.

Right before she turned to sit down, she saw someone in the corner of the bleachers holding a phone up. She saw long black hair behind the silhouette of the phone and her heart dropped.

She sat down with a thud and took a deep breath to focus. She did a mind jump to Booker and Dion. *"You guys were watching me right?"*

"Yeah," Dion responded.

"Of course," Booker said.

"Did I give anything away or did I look normal?"

Lanelle wished she could make the connection link so that Booker and Dion could hear each other and not just her. She just didn't have that much control yet.

"Yeah, you looked normal," Booker said.

"Why are you asking?" Dion responded.

She dared a glance backwards and saw Dion leaned over whispering something in Booker's ear.

"What's going on?" Dion asked.

Lanelle was getting so nervous she had to count to ten with deep breaths, in order to keep the link.

"I used my powers during meets and Michaelson is over there recording me."

Booker and Dion both leaned back on the bleachers and looked from one side to the other before spotting someone with big, rimmed glasses, long black hair. and a red coat with the color pulled up.

"She looks like a cartoon villain," Booker said.

If Lanelle wasn't panicking she would have laughed.

"*You looked normal Nelle, just don't use your powers on the next one.*"

The whistle blew and she lost her focus.

Won't it look suspicious if I slow down? She thought.

Lanelle stood up, it was time for the backstroke event. Lanelle walked to her position, taking deep breaths. She had not looked back towards Michaelson and it took everything in her to keep her head straight.

Once in position she looked towards her crew, partly because she needed some encouragement and partly as a distraction from looking at Michaelson. She landed on Jalen and he smiled and winked at her. She relaxed. The shot rang and she jumped into the water. The backstroke was not her best event, but she was still confident she was best on the team. She kept her mind free and clear. Jalen popped into her head and made her smile and then followed by the all too familiar guilt and she forced Booker into her head. She touched the wall and turned around and caught sight of someone a little in front of here.

All this thinking was messing her up. She tried to clear her mind and her fingers tingle with anticipation. Her wind was ready at her command. It felt like her body buzzed with disappointment when she didn't call it forward.

This is your happy place Lanelle. No one does the water like you do. She said as a mantra to herself. she popped up when her hands hit the wall and looked around. She'd come in second.

Her crew still lit up when she popped up. Whooping, hollering, and clapping. She dared a glance over in the direction of Ms. Michelson who had just lowered her phone and locked eyes with Lanelle. She winked as Lanelle glared at her.

Lanelle pulled herself out of the water and headed back to her spot. It was the boys turn and then she didn't swim until the freestyle round.

As she sat, she took a deep breath, mind jumping to her brother.

"Take out your phone and record me on the next one."

"Didn't I say don't use your power," Dion chastised.

"I didn't, but I want to see if I look different. I need to see me through her eyes. Just do it Dion," and then she broke the link.

On her final round Lanelle came through the winner. A whole five seconds before anyone else. She was so proud of herself and loved the validation that came with winning.

Heading back to her spot for the boys turn, she glanced and noticed Ms. Michaelson walking out the door.

All the satisfied feelings she felt a moment ago turned into dread. She counted the seconds until she could see Dion's video.

Sibling fighting x10

Lanelle groaned when she went back into the locker room and all her stuff was everywhere.

She glanced around quickly and then brought both her arms up. She began twirling them in circles and the contents of her bag lifted from the floor and began spinning it in circles. She quickly brought them from two rotating circles to one and then dropped everything in one pile.

"Nice trick," a voice said from behind her.

Lanelle froze and her blood turned to ice. Turning around, she pouted her lips and narrowed her eyes.

"What are you talking about? What are you even doing here?" Lanelle said to Michaelson.

"Should have had my phone out for that trick and not the boring swimming."

Lanelle kept her eyes narrowed and put her hand on her hip. "Can you go? I have a lot of homework to get done. Or do you not remember?"

Monica chuckled. "Poor baby. Homework keeps you from your boyfriend. I'm sure you can twirl your pencil up like you just did and make it done."

Monica stared Lanelle right in the eye waiting for her to respond. She wouldn't give her the satisfaction. "Whirl it around? How do you sound? I think being faced with your incompetence is getting to your head."

Monica's smile dropped. "You're going to tell me I didn't just see you push those papers and other crap around into one pile?"

"And how would I have done that?"

"With your magic, Dear," Monica replied.

Lanelle laughed "With my what? Did you just say magic? Listen Ms. Michaelson, I know this is a secret spy school and all but there is no such thing as magic. That only happens on TV."

"Don't try to play me for some fool child. I know what I saw. I saw those papers floating in midair. That's how she did it. You inherited it didn't you. Your, whatever you want to call it."

Lanelle placed both hands on her hip. She looked up to the ceiling and yawned feigning boredom. "Ms. Michaelson. I appreciate you coming to support the swim team and all. But I have a lot of work to do and do not have time to sit here talking about magic and floating papers with you. So, unless you have any proof," she waited a beat to see if Monica would offer her phone. "I would love to get on my way."

"Don't worry dear. The next I will be recording."

She turned and walked away without another word. Once Lanelle was sure she was gone she collapsed to the floor. She had fucked up. Michaelson knew about the magic. She pulled out her phone and texted Dion.

Lanelle: Come to my room ASAP!

She took a moment to compose herself and then picked her things up, putting them back into her backpack. Groaning, she realized she would have to go back to the library tonight to finish her homework.

* * *

Twenty minutes later, Lanelle came walking onto her hall.

Dion stood by her door. "How are you going to tell me ASAP and when I get here thinking you're dying or something got the nerve to not be here."

"I was coming from the pool," she said.

Dion frowned. "Why do you sound so, so, so exhausted?"

"I fucked up Dion," Lanelle said.

Now Lanelle cursed from time to time, but she never said the big-time curse words. She thought it was tacky and 'there were plenty other words to use.

"Whoa, you just cursed, what happened?"

"Michaelson saw me use my magic."

Dion's shock caused him to push the door with more pressure than he intended, and it slammed. He turned and looked at her. His eyes were stormy and she shrank back until her legs hit her bed. Plopping down on the bed she tensed and waited.

"Fucked up doesn't even cover it Lanelle," he scowled.

"I'll explain. Enough with the cursing. The point is made," she mumbled.

Dion's eyes widened. "How the fuck did you let her see you using your fucking magic Lanelle. The one fucking thing you were supposed to not fucking do, you do. Explain that shit to me please."

Lanelle's brows were furrowed. "Okay I get it. The language isn't necessary."

Dion threw his hands up "I don't give a fu -,"

Lanelle threw a ball of fire inches from his feet. He jumped back and yelled and then looked up at her, eyes narrowed.

"You know I don't like that language. The point was made not to stop it."

Dion made an icicle appear and threw it at her. She quickly put her hand up, melting the ice before it made it to her. She looked at Dion in shock.

"Two can play that game," He said as another icicle appeared in his hands. Lanelle threw a fireball at his hands, melting the ice but burning his hands in the process.

His rage exploded as he threw icicle after icicle at her. Lanelle couldn't melt them fast enough and became flustered.

She put both hands up, intending to ignite a big fire ball in front of her. Hoping to scare some sense into him. But instead the icicles started bouncing off of some invisible layer in front of her hands, hitting the ground with a thud but Dion kept coming at her. Getting closer and closer and throwing them harder and harder. She didn't know how she did this barrier and was afraid it would go away.

"Dion stop," she yelled. "You are trying to hurt me. Stop. Dion, stop."

She yelled it repeatedly until Dion had her slide her to the other side of her bed and she fell off the other side, hitting the ground with a thud. The barrier wavered, she saw it when the icicles hit it one after the other.

Unsure of what else to do, she took a deep breath and pushed her hands out along with all the energy she could muster.

Dion flew across the room and slammed against the door. Sliding down and hitting the floor with a thud.

Lanelle scrambled off the floor with tears streaming down her face. She ran over to Dion.

"*Booker,*" she mind jumped. *"Come here please, now."*

She crouched down in front of Dion and put her hand on his

chest. It was going up and down and she let out a deep breath. She pulled Dion's arm up and around her shoulders and tried to lift him up. She half dragged half carried him over to her bed. Halfway there, Booker came barging in.

"What the hell?" he said.

"Help me," Lanelle said straining.

Booker rushed over and lifted Dion off her shoulder.

He laid Dion down on the bed and then turned back to Lanelle. She had fallen in the middle of the floor and sobbed.

"Tell me what happened," Booker demanded.

Learned your lessons the hard way

Booker shook her. "Snap out of it," he demanded. "Tell me what happened."

Lanelle pushed him off her. Booker stumbled and raised his hands in surrender. "Okay, I'm sorry. But you need to tell me what happened. Do we need to call the nurse, your mother?"

Lanelle put her face in her hands. She crumpled on the floor as she continued to sob.

Booker went and sat on the edge of the bed. Thinking the best thing to do here was just wait. He turned and looked at Dion. He saw the rise and fall of his chest and knew he was breathing. But he didn't know what was wrong or what happened. He needed to know what to do next and for that, he needed Lanelle to tell him what happened.

"After swimming today, Michelson caught me in the locker room using magic," she said muffled, hands still covering her face.

Booker's head snapped towards her. He had so many questions at the tip of his tongue. How could she be so careless, stupid. He held them in, he needed her to finish.

After a few moments, she told him the events of the last two hours.

"It wasn't supposed to happen like that. He got so mad. He knows I do not like all the cursing. He knows I do not like all the cursing! Then it's like there was a switch in him. He completely flipped out. I wasn't trying to burn him. I flicked the fire as - a, as, urg, I don't know. But I've done it before in our arguments and he's never thrown those icicles before."

Lanelle looked at Dion, counting her breaths to make sure she took them. "This time was different. It was like, he didn't see that it was me. And, putting up that barrier did nothing but feed the rage he was feeling."

She blinked slowly and turned from Dion. "Booker, what do I do?"

Booker stared at her with wide eyes. He took a deep breath and opened his mouth. Only to shut it again. He did this three more times before he actually spoke. "I think you should call your mom."

Lanelle's head whipped up and Booker held his palm out. "The alternative is," he said quickly before she would refuse. "Telling someone at the school."

Lanelle put her head back in her hands and groaned.

After a moment, she pulled herself up and got her phone. Unlocking it she hit the duo app and held the phone up waiting for her mother to answer.

When Janelle accepted the call she was smiling, but quickly frowned when she saw Lanelle. "What happened?" she asked.

Lanelle looked at her mother and then up at the ceiling, blinking away the tears.

"Come on child, you're worrying me. What happened?" Janelle said with her Jamaican roots peeking through. She did a good job at hiding her accent, but it always came through when she was worried or mad.

Lanelle took a deep breath and relayed the story, again, of what happened. Janelle sat and listened intently. She had gotten Duante and set the phone up, so it saw both of them and she didn't have to hold it.

After Lanelle was done Duante asked her to show Dion on the camera so they could see him. He still was unconscious but was breathing.

"He might have a concussion," Janelle said. "We will have to take him to see his Dr."

She turned towards Duante "Honey, go call Dr. Andrews and tell him Dion possibly hit his head and when's the earliest time we can get it him in. When we have an appointment, I'll call Douglas and set up the away pass."

She turned back towards the phone. Lanelle was so nervous and scared she didn't know how to handle it.

"This is why we train," Janelle said to her finally. "This is why we tell you two not to use your gifts, especially on each other until you have more control. This is why we teach you how to harness your emotions to make them work for you and not run you. If you and your brother were in control of your emotions, this wouldn't have happened."

Lanelle lowered her head. "I know, I understand it now."

"I'm sure you do. Now," Janelle said, changing her tone. "We have some problems to solve huh? I need you and Booker, I know he's there right? Hello Booker."

Lanelle tightened her lips in embarrassment and Booker stood behind her on the camera.

"Hello, Ms. Sparks."

Janelle looked between the two of them with one eyebrow raised. "So, I need you guys to move Dion up, so he isn't hanging off the bed." Janelle looked at her daughter and saw the turmoil in her gaze. "Lanelle, he will be okay. Your power knocked him out. You had so many emotions adding fuel to your gifts they, like supercharged him. And when it hit him, it knocked him out. He will come back in time. In the meantime, though, he ain't got to be all hanging off the bed sideways," she added in an attempt at humor.

Lanelle's face cracked and a hint of a smirk seeped through. She put the phone down while she and Booker moved Dion to a more comfortable position. When she grabbed the phone again, Duante was back.

"Did he get an appointment?" she asked.

"Next one isn't for two days. So we will come out there to take him. He just needs someone checking on him throughout the night."

"We'll tell Imani, uh, something," Lanelle mind jumped to Booker.

"Okay, Booker will," She said to her parents.

Janelle and Duante gave each other a look of disbelief and then looked back at the camera.

"Let's talk about Monica. You said she saw you with your papers?"

Lanelle sat on the floor and crossed her legs. "That's what she said. I basically told her she was crazy and that she didn't have any proof."

"She will start following you now," Janelle said.

"She's been following me. She was at the swim meet. I swear she lives here. She did the count at like two in the morning."

Janelle frowned. "What count? A headcount?"

"Yeah, and she would have went in my room until the teacher who was with her said she isn't allowed to do that."

Janelle cursed under her breath. "Okay, I am going to need

you to read the handbook."

Lanelle furrowed her brows. "The handbook!" she exclaimed. "Why?"

"I need you to know the rules and what rights you have. This is not a request Lanelle."

Lanelle sighed and nodded her head.

"Monica is a good covert operative. She's good at not being seen. Don't underestimate her. She will be following you and you're not going to know it. That means you have to stop using your magic."

Lanelle frowned. "Doesn't she have to go home? I have to be on alert all the time, for what?"

"Because you got caught. She lives in one of the faculty provided housing on campus. So she will always be there."

Lanelle pouted but couldn't argue. She wasn't paying attention to her surroundings and, yeah, she got caught.

Janelle spent the next 10 minutes going between lecturing Lanelle, giving her advice on how to deal with Monica, and talking about Dion. Lanelle was exhausted when she hung up.

"I have a lot of homework I still need to finish," she said.

She looked around. Reading her mind Booker said, "I'll stay here with him and you can go to the library. If he wakes up while you're gone, I'll just take him downstairs."

Lanelle bit the side of her lip while she processed.

"Will you make up something to tell Imani, and she can stay with him, so you don't have to?"

"Yeah, I'll see you when you get back."

Lanelle gathered her things and headed to the door. She paused and looked back. "Thanks," she said and then headed out.

Damn

It's almost 6 o'clock when Lanelle walked into the library. She headed to the back, to her favorite booth out of the way facing the wall.

When she approaches, she realizes someone is there and pauses mid step. She spins around and notices for the first time that there are a lot of students here. The books, tables, chairs, everything is full. She turns and heads downstairs.

When her feet touch the bottom landing, she looks around and sees all the tables full. She walks in a little further to see if there are any in the back. All the tables have two people sitting them except one in the back.

Lanelle bits on her lower lip, anxious about asking someone she doesn't know to share a table.

As she approaches, she sees it's a boy, and he has dreads. She catches his profile; its Jalen sitting at the only table with space for her. With her phone in her hand as a disguise, she stands there awkwardly. Trying to figure out if she should just go to avoid sitting with Jalen.

Just as she is getting ready to turn and leave, he lifts his head. She should have spun and ran or hid her face, but she didn't. Something in her body stopped her from moving with the anticipation of seeing his face.

He smiled when he saw her and made a hand gesture for her to join him. She took a deep breath and walked to the table.

"What's up," he whispered when she got closer.

Lanelle waved, grabbed the chair next to him, and brought it the opposite side of the table. *As much space as possible* she thought.

Jalen smirked but didn't say anything. He watched her spread her things around the table. She leaned over and took her phone out of her back pocket and set it on the table next to her and started reading her textbook.

Lanelle tried hard not to glance up at him. Every time she did, he was looking at her. She swore the last time was the last time.

Her phone lit up on the table and she leaned over to see a message from Jalen. His bitmoji swinging on a vine. She chuckled quietly, sound coming out through her nose as she got back to work.

Over the next few hours, he kept sending messages to her phone, and staring at her. She looked up and noticed the crowd had died down. Checking her phone, she saw it was just past nine. *I should go check on Dion,* she thought.

"I'm done for the night. I'll see you around?" she asked and started putting her things together.

Jalen packed his things up. "Me too," he said. "I'll walk you."

Lanelle didn't see the harm in him walking her back to Howard. "Okay."

They walked back to Howard in comfortable silence.

"So, you're with that Booker kid huh?" he asked after a while.

Lanelle looked straight ahead, not wanting to make eye contact.

"Yup."

"Y'all together before here or," he faded off.

"We didn't know each other before coming here."

"So just since August then?" he asked.

"Yup," she answered. This was awkward, why couldn't they just continue to walk in silence. He never asked any more questions about Booker.

Instead, they talked about crap movies and how stupid trap music was. Well, Lanelle thought it was stupid. Jalen thought it was the best music since Motown. He lost some points with her on that.

By the time they got to Howard, Lanelle was laughing so hard she struggled standing up straight.

"Thanks for walking me," she said through gasps of air.

All he did was smile and wink at her before turning and walking away.

"Damn," was all she could say.

Lecture

When Lanelle entered the lobby she paused, debating on whether she should go see Dion or go straight upstairs.

She didn't want to be worrying all night, so she went to see Dion. When she got to his door, she knocked before she lost her nerve. Imani answered, her eyes wide when she saw Lanelle.

"There you are, he's been asking for you. You're not answering your phone."

Lanelle frowned and pulled her phone out of her back pocket. She had three missed calls from Dion. "Sorry," she shrugged. "My phone was still on silent from the library."

"You've been at the library all this time?" Dion asked as he sat up in bed.

"Uh, I'm going to get stuff from my room. I'll be back," Imani said and left before either one of them could respond.

Lanelle felt awkward and guilty as she stood by the door.

"Come here and sit down," he said.

When she sat on the edge of the bed Dion sucked his teeth. "Get up here," he gestured to the spot next to him.

She dropped her bag and kicked her shoes off before scooting to the top of the bed.

"I'm sorry," Lanelle said, eyes watering. "You scared me. I

didn't know what to do, I lost control."

She looked at him and then up at the ceiling, blinking the tears back.

"I don't know why I lost control," he said.

"I don't know what made me so mad. I guess I was just scared as to what having Michelson know about your magic meant."

They were quiet for a moment and Dion said, "I spoke with Ma and Pops. They gave me a lecture."

Lanelle huffed. "Yeah, me too."

Dion put his arm around Lanelle and she leaned in.

Monica Michelson

Over the next two weeks, Monica followed Lanelle around. The first week she thought it was a lost cause. She didn't do anything else magical.

Monica had heard of people before with magic, but she never believed them. She believed now, and she was sure the little winch inherited it from her mother.

The ceremony was on Saturday, which meant Monica had three days to compile all her video and slip it into the computer to play during the ceremony.

This past week Monica caught Lanelle making doors close without touching them, popping popcorn without putting it in the microwave, among other things. This was what she needed to ruin the Sparks and get their brats kicked out of Douglas, ending their stupid legacy line.

Monica opened the door to her classroom and yawned. She was tired. She had to re-do her whole plan because some of the kids complained about how much work they had to the Dean. She wanted to know who complained. What is it Lanelle? She was who all the work was intended for.

She went over to her desk and sat down. She cursed when she cracked her knee on the underside of the desk, trying to pull the chair up. She sat back and rubbed her knee.

Thank God, she didn't listen to her mother and wear stockings, those would have been ruined. She would have had to take them off anyway.

Her mind wandered to when Derek had her laid across this desk. He had made the comment of her not wearing stockings.

"Would have been sexy to peel them off of you," he said as he hiked her skirt up.

Monica was thrust from her thoughts by a knock at her door. As she stood up to go open it, it opened, and the Dean walked in.

Dean William Barkner was also the Director of the company. He spearheaded the merge of the two roles in his younger days because he insisted that the Director should have direct knowledge of the recruits.

"Dean Barkner," she said.

The Dean walked up to her and stood so close she felt his breath on the bridge of her nose. He reached up and slid his thumb down her cheek and she leaned into his touch.

"What brings you by this morning," she asked breathless.

The dean grabbed her by the hips and pushed her backwards, lifting her on her desk.

"Well sir, this I can accommodate."

Fair Trade

"She's a hoe," Lanelle said while her Booker, Dion, and Imani walked to class.

The two of them were behind Dion and Imani. "She has been doing Benjamin, and today the Dean!"

"I can't believe she doesn't know you are recording her yet," Imani said.

"It's just a listening device. Something happened this morning though because the signal went out for a minute. I'm going to have to go check it out." Dion said.

"Is that such a good idea?" Imani protested. "I mean, isn't the award ceremony Saturday? Can't we just use what we have?"

"After dinner today we can go back so I can check on the bug," Booker said.

Imani crossed her arms over her chest.

"Alright cool," Dion said.

"So, no one else thinks we already have enough," Imani demanded.

"If you two are going so am I," Lanelle said, ignoring Imani.

Imani huffed. "I'm not going. It's too risky."

Standing by the fountain, Imani and Lanelle go one direction for classes while Booker and Dion go another.

Imani said, "I don't understand why you all are messing with her anyway. You told the Dean about all the work she was giving. Doesn't that solve the issue?"

"She wants to mess with my mother getting the career award. We have to make sure that doesn't happen," Lanelle said. Leaving out the bits of information Imani didn't know.

"Your mama's grown, she can handle herself," Imani said.

"I always have my Mother's back," Lanelle said. "Period."

Imani rolled her eyes. "Whatever," she mumbled.

Lanelle sucked her teeth. "Listen I don't know your mother, since you never talk about your family. But I do know you have no right to sit there and judge me or my mother's relationship. I know she's grown. She is also not here and doesn't know what Michaelson is doing. I will not just sit back and let Michaelson's lies mess up my mother's name. So yes, I am going with the guys to look at the bug. I don't expect you to understand, just shut up about it."

Lanelle picked up her pace, jogging for the door. Leaving Imani in the standing there stunned. Her eyes began to water. "Maybe if I had a mother and not a grown daughter, I could understand the feeling," she mumbled.

* * *

After the academic buildings were closed Dion, Booker and Lanelle stood in front of Michaelson's classroom.

"When we get back, you need to apologize to Imani," Dion said.

"I am not. It's not my fault she got her feelings hurt. Next time she will keep her comments to herself."

"You don't know the whole story Lanelle," Dion said.

"That has nothing to do with me. She will never know about my magic and I will never know her secrets. Sounds like a fair trade."

Booker tried the doorknob and the door opened. They piled through the doorway and Dion went immediately to her desk and bent down. Looking under it, he cursed.

"What's wrong?" Booker asked.

"It's broken, that's why the signal messed up. It looks crushed."

"Just take it," Lanelle said. "We will use what we have. We don't have enough time to go find another one and put it in here."

Dion began yanking down the wires and froze. He tilted his head to one side. "Someone is coming. Hide."

The three of them scrambled and Dion and Booker managed to hide but as Lanelle turned to find another spot, she came face to face with Michaelson.

Back in the day

"What do we have here?" Michaelson said. "Funny, I forgot my video of your magic. The Dean said he would love to play my video collage of the family pictured at the ceremony," she said with one eyebrow raised and a smirk.

Lanelle's blood ran cold.

"I think everyone would love to see you opening doors without touching them. Oh, that popcorn trick, and," she placed her finger to her chin like she was thinking. "Oh, and that brother of yours making an ice pack out of thin air."

Lanelle's eyes narrowed and she glared at Monica, who only laughed. "What, nothing to say? That's uncharacteristic of you."

Lanelle put her hands on her hip. "I think I should go ask the Dean if I could add something. being her daughter, I am sure he would let me. The only question is, should I play the one of you and Mr. Benjamin or the one of Dean Barkner himself."

Monica's eyes narrowed and flew around her room. Checking the ceiling and all the nooks and crannies.

"There's a camera in here you little bitch?"

Lanelle's eyes got wide in mock offense. "Oh, I hope we got that. Calling children such vile names."

Monica stormed towards her and Lanelle got into her center position.

"What's going to light me on fire?"

"No, her mother is going to beat yo ass."

The light flicked on. Along with Booker and Dion being exposed, Janelle was standing there.

Lanelle's confusion showed on her face while Monica's eyes widened at the realization Lanelle was not the only one who was there.

"Moment of truth Monica. You've always said how better than me you are. Now is your chance. You can imagine how upset I was when I texted my son asking where they were at, surprise?? them. And to my disbelief he tells me he is hiding in Ms. Michaelson's classroom and she was confronting Lanelle with videos. They had no clue of course, that I was already on campus."

"You children have magic and I have it on video. I will expose them and you," Monica said, voice unwavering.

"That's fine, we will just say you photoshopped it or some-thing. In return, we will release our recordings. That my children took after I told them to leave you alone," she said, eyeing Lanelle.

Lanelle smirked and shrugged.

"So, you'll end up looking crazy and without a job. I bet Barkner doesn't know he's not the only one. Does he?"

"So we fight for it?" Monica asked, taking off her shoes.

"We can fight, sure. The end result is the same. Your video for mine. If you make me beat yo ass, then not only will I take your recording, I will send mine to everyone in the alumni network."

Janelle used her power to push the kids towards the door. Lanelle began to fight it at first but thought how it would look to Michaelson and decided against it.

"Shut the door," Janelle said when the kids were on the other side.

When she looked back to Monica, she had her shoes and jacket off and had rolled up the sleeves to her blouse.

"Okay, so we're doing this," Janelle said and attacked.

She ran at her and stopped last minute as Monica's foot went up in a straight on kick. Janelle went around her foot and punched her left. Monica squared off both feet and went around to kick Janelle in the ribs.

Janelle brought her knee to her elbow, deflected to kick and went to punch. Monica took the opportunity to kick a second time and caught Janelle in the ribs. Janelle grunted and staggered to the left, bent over slightly to catch her balance Monica jumped and kicked with her right foot, catching Janelle in the chin. Her head whipped back, and she hit the ground. Monica approached and kicked. Janelle caught her foot with both hands, twisting the foot hard, breaking the ankle.

Monica screamed in pain. Jenelle jumped to her feet and punched twice. Distracted, Monica was unable to keep her balance on one foot. Her head bounced back. Janelle jumped and kicked with her right, landing in her abdomen. Monica grunted and fell back hitting the ground with a thud.

Janelle wiped the blood dripping from her nose and she walked up to Monica.

She bent down. "Where's the damn video?"

Monica looked at her; nose bleeding, ankle broken and struggling for breath. "Flash drive in my desk drawer," she wheezed out.

Janelle rose to retrieve the flash drive and walked towards the door. "I assume you won't go spreading lies about my children?"

Monica wheezed. "Not lies, this is not over Sparks."

Lanelle burst through the door crying "Dean Barkner, Dean Barkner please help she's attacking my mother."

The Dean burst through the door and took in the scene. He looked at Lanelle. "You had nothing to worry about. I haven't met someone yet who could take down a take out a Sparks."

He looked over at Monica who was picking herself off the floor. "Barker, the kid is magic. I swear she is too. I have the kids on video. She has the recording in her hand. I have proof. I deserve that career award, not her."

The Dean put his finger and thumb at the bridge of his nose and squeezed. "There's a video?" he asked.

"Yes," Monica said.

Lanelle stepped forward and placed a phone in hands. "You can see it on here," Lanelle smirked. "I'm so happy you just happened to be in the academic building this late, Dean Barkner. It's such a coincidence."

Monica's eyes went wide. "No, she screeched. "Don't. That's not it, it's on a flash drive."

Then Sean looked at the phone, and down to Lanelle who smirked at him. He took a deep breath and handed the phone back.

"There is no such video, even if there was, it would not matter. Sparks has given years of her life to the company with great numbers and will still receive the award."

"No, the flash drive. William, the flash drive."

The Dean stared at her. "Changes are on the horizon, Michaelson. It seems you have become too used to your, um comforts here at Douglas. There is a transfer in your future."

Monica inhaled and held her hand to her chest. He began to walk away and she tried to follow him, but couldn't on her broken ankle.

"The nurse is on her way, get yourself cleaned up. We will talk in the morning. Goodnight children, Sparks."

Janelle smiled as she put her arm around Lanelle and walked towards Booker and Dion standing at the door. "Let's go find your Father."

"Right, where is Pops?" Dion said. "Could tell you did all the fighting back in the day, Ma."

Janelle chuckled. "Back in the day huh?"

About the Author

Indie Author | Bibliophile

Love reading? Have a huge TBR pile and still make it to the bookstore every day? Love it when you can get bargain books?

Sheyanne Warren is the author for you! She writes crime fiction, paranormal fiction, and Young Adult fantasy novels. A self-proclaimed bibliophile, she connects with readers, delivering new worlds and striking characters.

Sheyanne is a middle school teacher living in North Carolina, away from her home state New York. She has a Master's degree in Forensic Psychology, specializing in Juvenile Behavior.

She enjoys reading and writing, going on cultural outings such as museums, and loves history. Family is important and games nights, escape rooms, and movie nights are plentiful.

You can connect with me on:

🌐 https://foreversevenpress.com

🄵 https://www.facebook.com/swarrenauthor.indie

🔗 https://instagram.com/swarrenauthor

Subscribe to my newsletter:

✉ https://foreversevenpress.com